maya memory
The Glory That Was Palenque

Also by Dolly Calderon Wiseman

Everybody Eats Tortillas

maya memory
The Glory That Was Palenque

DOLLY CALDERON WISEMAN

BALBOA.
PRESS
A DIVISION OF HAY HOUSE

Balboa Press books may be ordered through booksellers or by contacting:

Balboa Press
A Division of Hay House
1663 Liberty Drive
Bloomington, IN 47403
www.balboapress.com
1-(877) 407-4847

Because of the dynamic nature of the Internet, any web addresses or links contained in this book may have changed since publication and may no longer be valid. The views expressed in this work are solely those of the author and do not necessarily reflect the views of the publisher, and the publisher hereby disclaims any responsibility for them.

The author of this book does not dispense medical advice or prescribe the use of any technique as a form of treatment for physical, emotional, or medical problems without the advice of a physician, either directly or indirectly. The intent of the author is only to offer information of a general nature to help you in your quest for emotional and spiritual well-being. In the event you use any of the information in this book for yourself, which is your constitutional right, the author and the publisher assume no responsibility for your actions.

Certain stock imagery © Thinkstock.
Any people depicted in stock imagery provided by Thinkstock are models, and such images are being used for illustrative purposes only.

ISBN: 978-1-4525-4206-5 (e)
ISBN: 978-1-4525-4207-2 (sc)
ISBN: 978-1-4525-4208-9 (hc)

Library of Congress Control Number: 2011919541

Printed in the United States of America

Balboa Press rev. date: 11/11/2011

For Brad

"Those who cannot remember the past are condemned to repeat it."

George Santayana

PREFACE

One morning in 1980, I awoke from the most realistic dream I had ever experienced. It was upsetting, yet intriguing. I wrote the dream down in my daily journal and marveled at the detailed images I remembered so vividly. My emotions were flowing. The descriptions of the people and of the palace where the dream took place were almost writing themselves. While I didn't know the time period or location, the dream's absolute clarity gave me the feeling this dream was a memory of a time long past. In this dream, I wore a long, white, lightweight gown, and I remember my bare arms and sandaled feet. I also remembered how the palace walls were made of stone and lit by torches. When I spoke in my dream, my present-day self was aware of a strange language I was speaking effortlessly—with lots of *sh, el,* and *kah* sounds.

As a modern, busy mother of three boys all under the age of eleven, my daily activities soon forced me to put aside any interest in my dream. However, in 1984, just for fun, I took a class in drawing for children's books at a local university. Our assignment was to illustrate an existing children's story or write and illustrate an original story.

Since I have always loved the beauty and grace of llamas, I decided to write a story for my sons about a little Inca boy and his llama and include original illustrations. As I sat in a local library looking for Peru in a book on the ancient Americas, my world changed. I came across a photo of the very place where my memory dream of 1980 took place: the ancient Maya city of Palenque, Mexico. I got the nostalgic feeling one has gazing at a photo of a childhood home. My memory dream of years earlier came flooding back, and with tears in my eyes, I almost murmured aloud, *"Aha!"* There in the photo was the palace colonnade where I had walked and the path my servant had carried me down to the valley! This was only the beginning of the mind-boggling discoveries that would follow.

Over the years, as I would read articles about the Mayas, I learned why the people in my dream were burning large bundles of dried cornstalks. I learned why I had looked up to the sky, knowing my future was to be read there. So much information verified events in my dream that periodically, I had to stop my research and look in wonder at the explanations in print detailing events I had already recorded many years earlier in my diary! My investigations were fascinating and triggered even more memories as I wrote.

For the past thirty years, I have collected magazine and newspaper articles concerning the ancient Mayas, hoping to find some clue as to why I had the dream that still remained as clear in my memory as if it had really happened. Family and friends encouraged me to write this book to find my answer.

The Dream Memory is the exact retelling of my dream in the first person, but embellished slightly by research. The fictional story that begins with Chapter One is told in the third person, and the storyteller becomes evident at the end of the story.

Today, thanks to many dedicated archeologists from all over the world, much additional research has taken place in Mexico and the Yucatan. I am now able to piece together memories, historical facts, and a little imagination to share this unforgettable experience.

My story takes place at the end of the Classic Era of Maya history during the ten-year period before the fall of Palenque in AD 879. New translations of Maya script show that the independent city-state of Palenque was originally called *Bak*, meaning "bone," and later called *Lakam Ha*, the Maya words for "big water." Currently called by its Spanish name, Palenque thrived as a prosperous hub of trade and commerce. For centuries, royal dynasties ruled over this teeming city of fifty thousand inhabitants, making it one of the most beautiful and successful monuments to the greatness of the Maya people. Tremendous strides in mathematics, astronomy, art, agriculture, and science were recorded there. Then, suddenly, the city was abandoned. What happened to this thriving metropolis and its inhabitants has remained a mystery to archeologists and historians. This once-great Maya capital was left to sleep under the safe blanket of the jungle for over nine hundred years.

In 1784, the Catholic church sent José Antonio Calderón, deputy mayor of the city of Santo Domingo del Palenque, located some seven kilometers from the ancient city, to look into the reports of "strange stone houses" which had been seen in the jungle as far back as 1746. Calderón made crude drawings of his find and sent them to Brigadier Josef Estacharía, who was appointed president and captain general of Guatemala by Charles III, King of Spain. Forty years later, at the command of King Charles and with Calderón's help, clearing of the area began, and reports were sent back to Spain. These documents were then filed away without much notice.

An American, John Stephen, and his associate, Frederick Catherwood of England, headed the first serious discovery and documentation of the ruins. They began with a minor excavation in 1834, eighty-eight years after José Antonio Calderón's first drawings of Palenque. Incidentally, my maiden name is Calderon. This is only one of the many incredible coincidences I have experienced on this journey of discovery!

Today, no one is certain of the reason for the fall of each of the great Maya cities, but weather changes, soil depletion, disease, and civil wars have been the most popular opinions. To date, no discoveries after about AD 799 are documented in Palenque.

What happened to the Maya people of Palenque? I know, for I was there. Come with me to the innermost corners of my dream to discover the secrets held by the last of the great Maya civilizations and to learn my *Maya Memory: The Glory That Was Palenque.*

ACKNOWLEDGMENTS

Thanks to my wonderful husband, Brad, who suggested I turn my memory dream into a book. Thank you for being there and reading my work from beginning to end. Family and friends convinced me to keep writing, even when I wondered why I had embarked on this journey. Thank you to my sons, Darren, Brandon, and Jason Boyd, who have had to listen to the retelling of my dream for as long as they can remember. My sons, along with Seth and Melissa Wiseman, have encouraged me all along the way. My cousin, Dr. Adelaide Randak, gave me helpful character advice and answered my medical questions. My cousin, author and educator Rebecca Morales, guided me to editor Susan Seteducato, who made me see my novel in a new light. I am grateful to archaeologist and Maya Exploration Center Director Dr. Edwin Barnhart of the University of Texas at Austin, who answered many questions about Palenque. I owe a debt of gratitude to my California Writer's Club critique group, who carefully suggested better ways to build my story. Thank you to author Diana Johnson, author and illustrator Howard Goldstein, and author Ester Shifren for your generous time and help during the crafting of my tale. I appreciate the help of Betty Spencer and the encouragement from The Ladies Who Lunch: Melanie, Lisa, Monica, and Hope, you are all goddesses.

Lastly, I thank my distant relatives who may have passed down the memories I experienced so many years ago. The dream I had and the words I wrote all came from someplace deep inside my memories. As the story spilled out, surprising me in many ways, there was no mistaking this tale shouted to me that it must be told. I hope at least one person will be moved to make a change to preserve the beautiful world we live in.

PROLOGUE

THE DREAM MEMORY
Palenque, Chiapas, Mexico, AD 879

I know my husband, the king, will die this night. For many days, he has been lost in the strange sleep that keeps him poised at the doorway to the next world. The room is silent except for his labored breathing. My heart aches for his struggle. I want to lie next to him, feel his strong warmth, and hear his assurance that he will take care of everything as usual. But I know that is never to be again.

I watch my hands as they arrange the assorted pottery vessels I had placed on a small table near him. I check each bottle, making sure the stoppers are secure, for they contain the magic liquid that numbs his pain. The burning incense pots do little to mask the overpowering, fetid smell of death here in his room. Fighting the urge to hold my breath and run to the fresh night air outside, I calm my mind and compose my face. Should he awaken, he will not see a hint of nausea on my expression or the sadness in my heart toward him for leaving me now.

The priests recorded that a great ball of light crossed the sky only twelve days ago, foretelling the death of the king. He looks frail and colorless—a shell of the great warrior I married ten *tuns* past. The light from the single wall torch throws deep shadows under his cheekbones and hollows his eyes. I close mine, remembering him in his gallant attire of jaguar skins decorated with shells and jade.

But now, in his seventieth *tun,* he lies here, barely able to breathe, his wasted body preparing to sleep forever. I glance at his old servant, Chan Och, nearly the same age as the king, as he lies asleep on a pallet in the corner of the sparsely furnished room. I thank the gods he will help care for the body of my husband. The old servant will observe the priests who carefully embalm the king's body and paint it with red cinnabar and resin to preserve it on its journey to the next world. Chan Och's last duty will be to give his own life when he lies down near the great man as the two of them are buried in the tomb already prepared.

"Good night, my husband. May you feel my love and devotion surround you on your journey," I whisper. Holding my head high, I walk out of the room and pray to the gods the king will pass peacefully to the underworld of *Xibalbá* this night.

Outside, I breathe in the fresh, cleansing scent of the warm night air. The colonnade, which sits atop a monumental tiered and stepped foundation, is open to the views of the brilliant, glittering sky and verdant valley below. As I walk slowly to my quarters, my mind is a jumble of concerns. Foremost in my thoughts are my two sons. When I last checked on them some time earlier, they had been asleep in their shared room, their servants asleep on the floor beside them.

What will I do when the great palace of Palenque is left to me? I am only twenty-seven *tuns* old. K'in Balam, my older son, is only eight *tuns* old and won't be able to ascend the throne for at least another five *tuns*. I will have to rule as regent for him, in spite of the wishes of the king's brother-in-law. I make a mental note to consult the priests again and to speak with my close friend, Keh Cahal, the king's captain and leader of our army. I thank the gods he has been my support and strength during this stressful time. I know I can count on Keh Cahal for advice whenever decisions have to be made concerning affairs of state.

Why am I so fearful? After all, other great women have been monarchs of Palenque: Lady Kanal-Ikal had ruled for one *baktun,* and the Great Lady Zak-K'uk was queen for three *tuns*. But that period was over two hundred *tuns* past. Much has changed about the sovereignty since then, and the people of Palenque are now uneasy. Our dour high priest is very concerned.

With each successive reign, more monuments had to be built to every new ruler, and each had to be larger and greater than the last. Since the foiled peasant uprising twelve *tuns* past, the priests convinced the king that more festivals must be added to the many sacred days.

Although temporary, these celebrations allow the people to forget about their difficult life of hard labor and the dwindling supply of food, as the increasing population drains our precious land. More wars must be fought to capture and replenish the supply of sacrificial victims for the festivals.

But tonight, this moment is mine alone. Bright lights from the valley below draw me to the balcony. It is comforting to see my people burning piles of old cornstalks as they chant into the night. Their ancestors have farmed this way for centuries. Those ashes will be mixed into the soil, allowing it to rest and rejuvenate for future planting. This is the dry season—the time of the harvest.

As I look skyward, it seems the stars above are also ablaze. My future—and the future of my people—is written there in the *tzab*, the great Rattlesnake Tail of stars in the sky. I make a mental note to consult with the high priest for his predictions in the morning. From the palace's four-story observatory, the tallest structure in the complex, the high priest spends hours deciphering the messages in the stars. I close my eyes and wonder, *Will I ever be happy again?*

A vague uneasiness interrupts my thoughts—a feeling I am being watched. I look around, but see no one. With an exhausted sigh, I turn toward my rooms. Besides the beetles singing in their twelve-tone harmony, the only sound I hear is the soft patting of my leather sandals on the polished stone floor of the colonnade. The uneasiness creeps up my spine once again, and I whirl to look behind me. Chukah Nuk T'zi, my personal servant, is peering at me from a dark doorway. *How long has he been watching me?*

With a touch of fear, I address him more brusquely than normal. "Chukah, I won't need you anymore tonight. You are dismissed!"

He bows, but makes no move to leave. *How unlike him to disobey me,* I think as I turn to hurry to the safety of my rooms. He has been my trusted servant since my first pregnancy and has never once disobeyed. Because of his tremendous size and supreme intelligence, Chukah Nuk T'zi had been chosen from the worker class for palace service. Although mute, he has a gift for knowing my every wish before I utter it. Over the years, he has been my servant I have rarely had to speak aloud to him;

it is as though he is a part of my thoughts. I know his giant body walks behind me now, and my strange fear becomes real. I turn to admonish him once more. "I said, you are dismissed!"

I approach the *Yax Tun*—the huge green boulder that dominates the colonnade. I place my hands on the ancient religious carvings inscribed on its face to steady myself. I have often wondered how a stone of such size was placed here. It stands taller than my height, and it would take four men with arms outstretched to encircle it. A thousand times, I have caressed the mysterious glyphs with their tales of famous leaders, extraordinary battles, important days, and ominous times to come. Although it stands between Chukah and me, it offers no safety, and no one else is nearby to hear me if I scream.

As Chukah comes closer, I know running or fighting is useless. I have never seen this strange look in his eyes or this determined set of his jaw. Now, too late, I realize I have accepted his servitude—his devotion—without question. I have never taken notice of his features before or thought to assess his considerable size. For the first time in all these years—perhaps because he has never been this close to me before—I notice his huge girth and his towering body. His tunic of coarse white fabric barely conceals the well-developed muscles of his enormous thighs and calves.

Within seconds, his face nears mine. I note his bold features—the dark slanting eyes topped by thick black bangs held down by a thin band, broad nose, and full lips. His shoulder-length hair swings into my face as he reaches for me with his curiously limp giant's hands. The rough material of his tunic scratches my skin as he picks me up gently but firmly, as though I am a small child in his huge arms. I regret wearing only my lightly woven white *po't* for sleeping. He lays me back on the slanted surface of the inscribed rock, the very rock that only today hid my youngest son from the older one as they played at an imaginary battle.

This cannot be happening to me! No ... I am your queen! Please, no! my heart cries out, but my tongue is silent. *My cries could bring my children, and they must not see me like this! Why is he doing this? I am not here ... I am watching my children at play ... I am walking with my sister ... Goddess Ix Chel, please help me!*

Steeling myself for the pain I expect from the size of his manhood, I turn away as he enters me, but to my amazement, I feel no discomfort. *Why is this?* His huge chest is close to my face. As I try in vain to push him away with my hands on his upper arms, I feel the odd texture of his skin—cool and firm, like the skin of the squash. *Chukah is not like us; his skin is of a different substance than mine! Who ... what is he?*

His body movements quicken, and my mind reaches for a safe place—any place but here. Grasping my memory for what the priests have taught me about the beginnings of the great Maya people, I remember the teachings.

The gods made four attempts at creating perfect human beings. The first attempt at crossbreeding with animals did not work, nor did the second attempt to create man from mud. The third attempt with wood was futile, as these people were wicked and could not bow to the gods. Most of them were annihilated by black rain and floods sent by the god Hurahkan, and the rest fled to the jungle to become monkeys. Finally, the fourth attempt succeeded when the gods created man by mixing their blood with the sacred cornmeal, and the great Maya race was born. As my slave holds me prisoner, I wonder, *Is Chukah Nuk T'zi an ancestor of the past attempts at humanity?*

He groans quietly and is finished with me. The giant looks down at the stone floor, almost afraid to return my angry stare. I regain some queenly composure, but I am still frightened and enraged at what has happened and glare into his tear-rimmed eyes. He is obviously sorry for what he has just done.

For the first time since I have known him, mute Chukah speaks. "This was fated." His deep voice is barely a whisper as he gestures toward the valley. "Your life will now take place down there."

What does he mean? My mind races with arguments, but I know with all of my heart I cannot stay in the palace. I could be killed or sacrificed for my actions even though I am not a willing participant. The priests will know what happened here tonight; they can divine anything. My mind flies to my sons. *My sons!* Perhaps I can escape with them in the morning! I can't ask them to live with my humiliation. Had the gods planned this even before I came to Palenque ten *tuns* ago?

Something inside me dies. I become numb and resigned to my fate as Chukah gently lifts me into his huge arms and carries me down the dozens of steps to the valley below.

"You are to be the mother of the new race," he solemnly declares. "This was written."

From his arms, I turn to look back up at the palace that had been my home for so many years. I know now that tonight will be Palenque's collapse, just as other cities have fallen around us. The workers were waiting until now to make their move. Their happy singing in the fields was in anticipation of their attack on the palace, not cheerful workers harvesting the corn as I had earlier surmised. Chukah did that unspeakable act to get me away from the palace and to begin a different life for the Maya people. I feel the chill of truth over my body.

I am certain my husband will die peacefully tonight. My sons—potential monarchs and therefore a threat to the people who want freedom—will be murdered in their sleep, and the workers will overrun the palace, causing chaos unknown in those walls. The unsuspecting priests, servants, and guards will all die without ever knowing that I, their queen, was being carried to a new life with the Maya people: a life that had been planned long before—and that is far beyond my power to change.

CHAPTER ONE

AD 869
Ten years earlier

Lady Chanil Nab Chel felt older than her seventeen *tuns* as she was solemnly carried toward the beautiful city of Palenque. She sat atop an elegantly carved mahogany litter draped with a finely-woven fabric meant to shield her from the ever-present insects of the jungle. The young woman felt warm and uncomfortable. Her lightweight, sleeveless white ceremonial gown was topped with a heavily woven collar of brilliant threads chosen to imitate the sacred *k'uk* feathers. Adding to her burdensome costume were the weighty jade earplugs, jeweled wrist cuffs, and the belt she received from her husband-to-be. Her long black hair had been painstakingly dressed in the high fashion of the times: pulled straight up and back and tied in square portions to reveal her beautifully slanted forehead and high cheekbones.

Lady Chanil left her home in Tikal to become Second Wife to Palenque's high king. Troubling dreams had disturbed her nights, and apprehension filled her days as she traveled through the hot and humid orchid-filled jungle. Her retinue had journeyed for nearly twenty *k'in*. At times, the route took them on rivers where they boarded *kayuks* or on narrow jungle trails and often on the outskirts of cities in an effort to travel uninterrupted—and it was perhaps safer. The long trips each day would have been unbearable but for the many jaguar skin pillows stuffed with the silky fibers of kapok which were placed about her for her comfort. Any observer would note that a personage of great importance was headed for Palenque.

Heralding this colorful parade's progress were the sounds of howling monkeys and screeching parrots. Lady Chanil was surrounded by soldiers, priests, and various officials, all wanting to be part of the fantastic procession set up by her future husband, Lord Akal Balam. Dozens of porters carried the gifts of carved and polished jade jewelry, alabaster vases, rare shells, and hematite mirrors backed with mother of pearl. The finest textiles of Tikal were rolled on long poles. Added to these gifts were sacks of salt, sugar cane, cocoa beans, and ceramic jars of honey. The priests had calculated this day as the most auspicious time on the Sacred Round Calendar. Indeed, it had proven perfect for her entry into Palenque and the lives of its fifty thousand inhabitants.

The pageant had begun in her birth city of Tikal, also known by the ancient name of Mutul, and slowly wound its way down the sacred *sacbé* road of white stones. Workers from Palenque and neighboring cities had toiled for months in the humid weather to lengthen and flatten the road by rolling huge boulders over the smaller stones, thereby creating a dry route between the two cities. These peasant workers would be rewarded for their hard labor by joining in the celebration of the marriage of the Woman of Tikal and their king. This marriage would form an alliance between the two powerful cities, bringing an end to the constant threat of war.

Lady Chanil understood the marriage ceremony would take place immediately upon her arrival in Palenque. It was explained to her that Lord Akal's dramatically staged entrance of the new queen into the city was as important to the king as his own grand appearance in front of the populace as he greeted her. King Akal Balam of Palenque would appear in all his splendor at the steps of the Great Temple. There, in the grand ceremony, he would appeal to the gods for a long marriage and a fertile queen.

Runners from Lady Chanil's party told their retinue that the city teemed with anticipation. Even the constant building of temples had temporarily stopped, and all the people were put to work readying Palenque for the celebration. Peasant women applied a fresh coat of red ochre and other accent colors of bright blue, green, and yellow pigments on the impressive edifices lining the ceremonial route, and children decorated the temple steps with flowers. For the wealthier visitors and city inhabitants, chefs had been cooking the meat from the many animal sacrifices that had been performed over the past several days. They also displayed dried meats, such as rabbit, iguana, fowl, and pig, preserved in ground chili powder. In the main plaza, many *ploms* had set up their woven and pottery wares for barter. Musicians played their clay pipes and wooden flutes or beat their tortoise-shell drums with polished deer antlers. Local farmers had set up their stands with fruits, vegetables, and fish to feed the hundreds of people who had come from near and far for the celebration. This was to be the biggest event the people of Palenque had ever experienced!

As the temperature rose on the morning of the last day of travel, Lady Chanil was relieved she was not allowed to have her sister or her female servants sit with her; she needed time to herself. Her sister, Sak Ayi'in, chattered constantly, and her worry about life in the new palace had been tiring. Although the politics of palace life were familiar to Chanil, she knew no one in Palenque and had been glad she was permitted to bring people with her she knew well and could trust.

Her priest, Uncle Men Lamat, intruded upon her thoughts as he walked alongside her litter. "It is likely people from the city or spies of the palace have ventured into the jungle to hide and observe their new queen, only to brag to others they were the first to glimpse The Woman of Tikal," he confided. "It is important that you look as queenly as possible and go over in your mind the prayers and memorized responses we have been practicing these past three days. It will all be over soon." With that, he straightened his crooked, old back to look as holy as possible to any outsiders and marched on ahead of her.

Chanil wondered about the new life her other uncle, the King of Tikal, had bargained for her, but she was interrupted once again.

"My Lady," called out Keh Cahal, the king's war chief sent to lead the bridal procession. This handsome *nacom* was of medium height and had a broad chest and piercing stare. He quickly averted his eyes in respect and continued, "We are nearing Palenque. If you look above the trees, you will see the Great Temple where your marriage to our noble king will take place. I am honored to be war chief to King Akal Balam and equally honored to lead you here to Palenque." Immediately, he strode on ahead, shouting orders to his men to look smart and make their king proud. Chanil noticed how confidently the king's emissary carried himself. It was clear he cared little for the ornaments most men of high office wore to identify their rank and importance. She wondered if this man cared for a woman with as much fervor as he displayed for his king.

As the jungle began to thin, small, thatched peasant huts appeared, and the forested land gave way to fields of corn, beans, squash, and sugar cane. The finer stone houses of the city's elite soon replaced the poorer huts. Chanil knew they were nearing their destination, and her heartbeat quickened. Her retinue stopped momentarily as her maid tied the bride-to-be's huge headdress on, and Chanil and her sister hugged quickly. She looked about for Uncle Men Lamat and smiled in relief as he approached to take her hand.

"You look like a queen already, my sweet Chanil. Don't be nervous; you'll be fine." He patted her hand and took his place beside her litter.

As they approached the center of Palenque, the palace called *Bak,* with its four-tiered tower, dominated the city. Her new home atop its man-made escarpment looked like a red shining jewel in a green forest sea. It was truly a breathtaking sight. Uncle Men Lamat had told her that from its highest point, one could see all the way to the ocean in the north. It was obvious to Lady Chanil that the architects of Palenque had planned the palace and its temples as a backdrop for public ceremonies such as this. Red stucco plaster coated the royal building's facade. Paintings of honored kings and queens in blue and yellow were polished to a sheen on its walls. Although Lady Chanil was transfixed with the beauty of Palenque, she gazed with apprehension out over the throngs of cheering peasants and unfamiliar faces.

"Welcome, new queen!" they yelled. "May you bring us an heir!" others shouted.

The procession passed the palace, which was the residential and administrative complex for the city, and ended at the steps of the Great Temple that housed the burial chamber of Palenque's greatest king, Lord

Pakal. The elegant and lofty roof crest made the building appear to be one half again as tall as it actually was. Large and splendidly painted censers depicting gods and Palenque's past monarchs lined both sides of the steps to the temple. They all faced west and burned with copal, giving the air a dizzyingly sweet aroma.

It sounded as though a hundred drums began to beat as two elder priests emerged to guide Chanil's litter, carried by four strong, young priests up the sixty-nine steep steps to the elegantly decorated platform high above the crowd. The cheering was deafening as she was placed to the right of the center doorway.

The tall and very thin high priest, Ah Kan Mai, appeared resplendent in his brilliantly feathered *patí*—a cape with feathers from every type of bird in the jungle—and skirt of jaguar skins. His glaring stare made her feel as though she were naked in front of these thousands of strangers. The high priest raised his arms skyward, and a hush fell over the crowd. He blew into a huge spiraled conch shell three times to call forth the triad of gods who ruled so favorably over Palenque's people.

At that moment, her future husband, Lord Akal Balam, appeared from the temple. She felt her breath catch at the splendor of the great man to whom she would pledge her life that day.

His headdress, made of carved and painted palm wood and the long feathers of the revered and rare *k'uk* bird, glistened in the sun. It made him appear to be half again taller than his already considerable height. He wore huge earplugs that dangled to his shoulders and a clay nose bridge pressed over his own nose to enhance his noble profile. A heavy carved jade necklace accentuated his bold face, and a sleek jaguar-skin tunic hung from his waist to his thighs. Under his tunic was a knee-length skirt of the finest white linen woven with gold-colored threads, and he wore intricately stitched deer-hide wrist and ankle cuffs. Completing his costume, the jade and obsidian jewelry on his arms and fingers shone as brilliantly as the sun, from whence all Maya people believed he had descended.

Lady Chanil stepped down from her litter and approached the impressive king who would shortly become her husband. He smiled momentarily to reassure her, but their attention was quickly averted to the high priest. He draped the king and new queen in their matrimonial robes, which were beautifully decorated with matching feathers and pearls and edged with hematite mirrors adorning the front and hems. They turned to the cheering crowds and then faced the priest. The king smoked the ceremonial cigar offered to him by Ah Kan Mai and passed it to Chanil. Within moments, the hallucinogens began their sacred work.

In a deep, melodic voice, King Akal prayed for a long and fruitful marriage, then took the royal perforator from the high priest and held it high in his right hand for all to see. He sat on a carved stone bench with his left foot drawn near to his body. With his left hand, he parted his tunic, grasped the tender foreskin beneath his penis, and deftly plunged the obsidian dagger through it.

Numb to pain from the cigar's powerful drug, he passed a stingray spine through the wound. The king reeled in his trance as his spirit descended to the underworld and then up to the heavens. He stood and squatted to catch the blood from his scrotum as it dripped onto the sacred bark paper he held between his legs. King Akal then pleaded with the gods to bless this day and bring the next great Maya ruler through this union.

Lady Chanil Nab Chel recited her memorized prayer to the gods for their blessing. Having already smoked the same cigar as the king, she kneeled before her new husband and handed him her perforator as she extended her tongue. She ran her thorn-laced rope through the wound he had made, allowing her blood to drip onto the bark paper in the same *lac,* the sacred offertory bowl before her.

The high priest held the blood-soaked papers high above his head for all to see before he placed them again in the *lac* containing copal incense, rubber, and wood. With a flourish, he lit the holy fires that would send their mixed and burning blood skyward to nourish the gods. Then he took the inside front corner of the hem from each of the royal couple's cloaks, tied them together in a knot, and pronounced that the gods were indeed pleased with this union. Ah Kan Mai blew the conch shell again to announce the marriage ceremony over. It was time for the festivities to begin.

Shouting, the people began to rejoice. They hardly noticed their new queen had disappeared into the temple after her husband, who had been whisked away to recover from his sacrificial duties. Queen Chanil Nab Chel wrapped her tongue with the soothing herb-soaked cloth given by servants and wished to be home again in Tikal.

Her new life had begun as consort to the king of one of the greatest cities of the Mayan Empire.

CHAPTER TWO

High Priest Ah Kan Mai did not plan to make life easy for the woman of Tikal. He was against this marriage, and the wedding festivities were beginning to bore him. As he watched her meeting the *sahals*—the regional governors and their families—he remembered how the king had been enchanted by her beauty during the time they visited Tikal for the last *yahau*, the convening of the council of kings.

King Akal had seemed more interested in the young noblewoman than in the important discussions that had to take place concerning trade between the city-states. The high priest didn't think her so attractive. But now, he had to admit she carried herself with dignity as a noblewoman would and performed her first duties as the king's wife flawlessly. Although her eyes were large and almond-shaped, they did not please his standard of beauty. *The people may find her flawed. When she was an infant, her parents did not correctly train her eyes to cross inward enough to truly call her beautiful,* Ah Kan Mai decided.

He remembered the king's enthusiasm as Lord Akal confided to him the last day of the *yahau*. "Lady Chanil Nab Chel descends from the best line of nobility in Tikal. After all, her uncle *is* the king. She has skin like mother-of-pearl, and her height allows her to stand head-to-head with me. Since she truly is as beautiful as the water lily and rainbow she was named after, I think she will bring me handsome heirs and produce an intelligent and noble king to rule Palenque when I am gone. And because there are *twice* as many people in Tikal as there are in Palenque, I think it is best we remain friendly with them!" the king proclaimed as he roared with laughter that day.

If the new queen plans on wielding her beauty and power over me, I shall have to put her in her place, thought Ah Kan Mai as he surveyed the wedding celebration. *She has come to halt the threat of war with Tikal, yes—but she will also take the seed of our great* halach uinic, *our hereditary ruler! We could have had another queen from our own line—one who was descended from our own past kings, just as the First Wife is. But now that the old queen suffers from bone disease, Lord Akal Balam has taken this younger woman. Her appearance here is only a slight inconvenience.*

Yet just as I finally have all of the palace priests now doing my bidding, she has brought in a formidable old priest from Tikal. I will have to be very careful around him for the time being. This woman has come from our ancient enemies who once warred with Palenque. But since the kings decided to divide all of the Maya lands equally into city-states, Tikal is as busy with its responsibilities as we are with ours. For now, I will see to it this woman of Tikal will not feel welcomed here.

Planning how to best rid Palenque of the intruder would be a delicious diversion for him. Usually, he achieved sexual ecstasy during his sacrificial and bloodletting duties as high priest, but the old excitement was beginning to wane lately. Just thinking of the new queen's suffering began to arouse him as he imagined her supple young body lying on the sacrificial altar, her clothes torn from her breasts, and her milky-white skin exposed to his blade. No drug in his vast stores could compare to the delirium he was beginning to feel.

Ah Kan Mai quietly slipped away from the wedding banquet and headed for his sanctuary—his tower of potions and incense.

Having no family and having been brought up in the priesthood as a child, Ah Kan Mai had no close attachments and generally disdained anyone he considered beneath him. As a highly intelligent and observant man who had been Palenque's high priest for twenty *tuns,* he was aware of the forces changing his beloved city. He barely hid his contempt for the lower intelligence of the other priests. Ah Kan Mai believed he was the only savior of Palenque.

Drug-induced trances brought Ah Kan Mai dire predictions for the future. Only last night in his visions, his spirit animal guide—his *uay,* the snake—had shown him his royally clothed king with elaborate headdress being wholly engulfed by an enormous boa constrictor. The snake, whose body was distended with Lord Akal inside, convulsed and then excreted a large pile of smelly *ta'* which turned into millions of tiny snakes.

He then saw the new queen holding a newborn son whose umbilicus entwined with the smaller snakes. Those snakes became vines of the jungle and pursued the larger snake. In his vision, Ah Kan Mai picked up a stoneworker's *bat,* and with this axe, began chopping at the vines as he cut off the head of the large snake, its frightful fangs still biting at an unseen enemy.

Why would his snake guide give him this disturbing premonition? *It must mean I will be the one to protect Palenque from such a future. But I will need more allies in the palace.*

The day after the wedding, Ah Kan Mai took a trip to the limestone quarries. Perhaps the reason for the stone-cutting *bat* in his vision could be found in the valley of Palenque's finest limestone. His premonition was correct. There, he encountered a giant of a man honing stone blocks for the new temple to the rain god. This huge worker was as tall as the palace doorways, as strong as six men, and moved like a jaguar. He didn't look like a Maya man, but more like the ancient Olmec people. The foreman explained that although the man was mute, he was a good and reliable worker.

Brute strength and lower intelligence is just the sort of help I could use in the palace, and his silence is a gift of the gods. Finding this giant honing limestone for the new temple to the rain god Cha'ac is surely an auspicious omen!

Although the priest feared that *K'awiil,* the god of lightning and sexual release, might be displeased at his taking away a valuable worker on the rain god's temple, he would surely be satisfied this worker would be in palace service. Perhaps the god would be so pleased he would restore to Ah Kan Mai, his obedient servant, the lust and sexual ecstasy that had lately diminished. The priest had even taken to wearing a cord over his groin that held the much-prized pink spondylus shell from the fluid and fertile ocean—but to no avail.

Observing how the giant's huge hands expertly wielded the *bat* to shape the temple's block walls was awe-inspiring. The priest felt a tingle of fear. Reminding himself the gods were the only ones to be feared, Ah Kan Mai approached the man and commanded, "Kneel in front of me, slave!"

As soon as the big man's face was close to the earth, the priest continued, "From today onward, you owe me your life, as I have just saved you from certain sacrifice. I am bringing you to the palace, and there you will obey only my instructions. Do you understand?"

Ah Kan Mai's onyx black eyes penetrated the back of the giant's head as his voice pierced the air again. "I don't know what your name is, and I don't care, for at this moment, I am renaming you Chukah Nuk T'zi to remind you that you are nothing more than a large captured dog in my estimation. Now follow my litter back to the palace."

The high priest hissed commands to his slaves and looked back to smile as he observed the giant quickly drop his tools on the ground and fall in behind Ah Kan Mai's regal retinue.

An older worker clenched his *bat* tightly as he watched the monstrous man follow the priest in the direction of the palace. The giant's adoptive father, Moch Chuen, wondered if he would ever see his son again. He would have the palace servants watch his activities and report back to him about how his son, now called Chukah Nuk T'zi, was being treated.

His adoptive son was a gift from the gods. Moch Chuen remembered the day many *tuns* ago when he had taken a short-cut home on a trail through the jungle. Besides the howling of monkeys and screeching of parrots, he heard another sound—that of an infant crying loudly. There in a clearing, he found a baby—a large baby—wrapped in coarse blankets howling so loudly, the man wondered why a jaguar hadn't also heard the baby's cries and come to feast on the chubby infant squirming on the jungle floor. He knew the gods had sent this child to him and his wife, who had just lost their little girl in sacrifice to that animal, the high priest Ah Kan Mai. This boy was to be theirs—a big, strong boy who would work with his father and take care of his new parents when they reached old age. They named him K'a'an K'aax Paal, for he was truly a strong forest child.

But now, the high priest had taken his second child and given him a new name so that he would be reminded daily he was no longer Moch Chuen's boy. The older worker resumed his work with hate for the high priest fueling his every strike at the dry limestone.

Once at the palace, attendants dressed the giant man in a coarsely woven tunic; shoes to fit his huge feet would take time to be specially made. In the meantime, he could go barefoot, as he had as a quarry worker. Without protest or question, Chukah Nuk T'zi began the new life that would seem as far from his simple and happy peasant's life as the stars are from the moon.

CHAPTER THREE

The king was an imposing man, and although he was old enough to be Chanil's grandfather, his long, thick black hair and lean, muscular body made him look younger than his sixty *tuns*. Determined to allay his new bride's matrimonial fears, he handled her gently and lovingly on the night of their marriage.

"My Dearest Chanil, you may feel awkward with me. Although I am much older than you, I understand what you might be experiencing. I promise to be gentle and will stop if you are feeling uncomfortable. We have the rest of our lives together, so although my body can't wait to cherish you, my heart can resist until you desire me as much as I do you. Your body is beautiful, and I promise never to force myself on you."

Chanil's initial apprehensions dissipated almost immediately. She began to feel safe in her husband's arms, and her loving and generous nature made her want to please the king. Being in Akal's arms brought back the comforting feelings of being a little girl again in her father's protective embrace.

Right away, Chanil became as relaxed in his rooms as she was in her own quarters, even though his brightly colored suite adjoined that of the First Wife. Chanil was intrigued by his tables of war trophies laden with shells, crystals, pottery, and jewelry. Particularly fascinating were the pieces of rare, finely tooled gold from cities far to the north. She immediately became comfortable with Chan Och, the king's old servant, who had been in his service for some thirty *tuns*.

Akal enjoyed his new wife's refreshing versions of palace life as she recounted events of the day. He looked forward to her descriptions of lengthy sessions with the aged priests who took it upon themselves to educate her on palace policies. He laughed hardest at her imitation of Ah Kan Mai imperiously ordering palace servants to do menial tasks and punishing them for the tiniest infringements of palace etiquette.

As Chanil and her sister, Sak Ayi'in, walked together near their rooms, Chanil was brimming with excitement.

"The palace is still celebrating my marriage, Sak. As part of the welcome festivities, a ball game is scheduled this afternoon. Please sit with me? It will be exciting!" Chanil took her sister's hand. "Come, let's prepare our clothing for this grand event."

"I wonder if it is played the same way as it is Tikal, Chanil," Lady Sak said. "I love seeing those handsome athletes hitting the ball all around the court. They're so strong!" Lady Sak giggled. "It will also be interesting to see who from the palace will be in attendance."

Chanil was offered seating to the right of the king's chair, with her sister next to her. Hundreds of the elite and their families were already seated, busy chatting with friends, and looking around to see who else was there. The spirit of excitement permeated the air.

"Look, Chanil … it's the First Wife and her daughter!" whispered Lady Sak, pointing in the direction of the royal access to the upper left of the court.

Making a grand entrance, the First Wife waved to the cheering crowd. It was obvious the old queen was well loved by the throngs of citizens. Lady Zac Ku stopped to acknowledge the many *sahals* and their families she had known over the years. Her daughter, a rather stout younger woman, and her thin husband followed the older queen to their seats. The First Wife nodded a curt greeting to Chanil before she sat on the opposite side of the king's seat to his left. Her daughter and son-in-law seemed not to notice Chanil's existence.

King Akal entered the seating area. The people of Palenque rose to their feet to shout and hoot for King Akal as he walked to his bench in the center of the audience. Chanil felt as excited as the citizenry upon seeing Akal. He took the First Wife's hand and bowed slightly to her. He then walked to Chanil and took her by the hand, encouraging her to stand. He raised both his arms up in victory, still holding her hand as the people in the crowd cheered their new queen.

Almost as wild as the shouts for the king were the whistles and yells for the eight ball players as they marched in and stood in teams of four on either side of the oblong sunken ball court. The athletes looked imposing in their uniforms: colorful vulture headdresses on one team and deer headdresses on the other. Thick padding, called *hachas,* protected their hips, knees, and forearms, and leather skirts added to their impressive costumes. As soon as the priests offered prayers and incense to the gods, an expectant hush fell over the audience. The game began.

One player set the melon-sized rubber ball in motion as he threw it in the air and struck it with his padded hip. A teammate attempted to hit the ball with his thigh through the carved stone goal ring projecting from the wall of the court. But an opposing team member shot forward with jaguar speed and slammed the ball away with a padded shoulder. The crowd went wild! Over and over, the players guarded the goal rings and struck the ball in different directions.

"Chanil, now that it is the dry season, our young *pitzlawal* are competing in my favorite sport. I know both of Tikal's *pitz* courts are larger than ours, but our games are exciting, aren't they?" The king shouted to be heard above the noisy crowd. "Our best athletes shine against our captured enemies!"

And indeed the local team won. In a solemn parade, the losing team walked behind their captain to Ah Kan Mai, who stood at one end of the ball court. As the captain kneeled in front of the priest, lower priests removed his headdress, padding, and earrings.

In one deft blow, Ah Kan Mai beheaded the athlete, and the crowd stood with a deafening roar.

"Although I am fascinated by the game, I can't understand the reason for sacrificing the captain of the losing team at the end of every game. What a pity the lives of talented young athletes are destroyed in their prime," the young queen commented to Akal. "If they weren't sacrificed, the same popular team captains could go on to play *more* exciting games!"

The king agreed. "One team is bound to lose in spite of the enemas of sacred mushrooms which heighten their reflexes and coordination. This is our tradition, Chanil."

"Just as my uncle does in Tikal, I suppose you often take the position of captain and, of course, always prevail over the opposing team in a display of good triumphing over evil."

"It may seem barbaric, Chanil, but that is how we appease our people," the king answered her. "Our citizens place bets on their favorite teams, and as you have witnessed, the winners leave with the approval and much of the jewelry of the spectators. Our ball games are important, and so are our traditions." The king stood and began walking out of the arena stands. Lady Chanil followed him with her sister close behind.

"Just as in Tikal, we honor our religious and city holidays and dedications of new buildings. When we war with a neighboring city-state, there are celebrations and games both before the war and afterward. Along with dancing and dramatic performances, we must have our important human sacrifices. These offerings of slaves, orphans, and prisoners send the human energy skyward and keep the cosmos in balance, Chanil.

"More and more public events are required to keep the people preoccupied. Their undercurrent of agitation is evident to only a few of us," the king said, losing his jovial mood. "Let us go back to the palace now," he muttered, and he strode on ahead.

The young queen turned to her sister. "Can you feel the king's uneasiness, Sak? There is an air of disquiet in this place." She linked her arm with her sister's as they walked. "I have much to learn of my new city and its people."

CHAPTER FOUR

Queen Chanil stood at her window the next morning waiting for Uncle Men Lamat and looked at the busy courtyard several steps below. Gardeners bustled about, pruning and replanting. Women swept walkways, and workers repaired stucco. Her rooms were small but lovely, and the red walls were accented with painted flowers in an array of colors. Her servant, Muluc, parted the doorway curtains to announce Men Lamat's arrival.

"Come in, dear Uncle. I have pots of cacao ready for your visit," she said, welcoming the old priest into her quarters. Muluc immediately set an empty cup on the floor. The young servant raised a cacao pot as high as her arms could reach, tipped it, and expertly poured a stream of cacao directly into the cup, producing a high froth at the top of the liquid. She handed the drink to Men Lamat, bowed, and quietly left the room.

"Thank you, my dear," Men Lamat called to the departing girl. "Now, Chanil, I know we have only been here a few days, but I am concerned about how you are adjusting to your life as a newlywed and queen in a foreign city. How has your reception been in your new home?"

"As expected, I am shown courtesy by the palace attendants. But I know they are listening to every conversation between Sak Ayi'in and me," she whispered, thinking of how her door barriers—screens of wood-framed, brightly woven linen on wooden stands—gave her rooms a sense of privacy, especially at night.

"There are always several bowls of floating water lilies to grace my table tops. See how elaborately these vases are painted with scenes of life at court? They are constantly filled with freshly cut orchids and placed about my rooms. I am happy with the easy access to the labyrinth of passageways throughout the palace. I readily discovered the halls leading to my steam bath, my latrine, and patios. Thankfully, I am close to Sak Ayi'in's rooms and to your personal quarters below, dear Uncle.

"Yet I feel a chill go up my spine whenever I am around the high priest, Ah Kan Mai. I feel death around him. Perhaps I sense the anguished souls of the hundreds of people he has killed over many *tuns* in his frequent sacrificial ceremonies. His gaunt skeletal face is frightening. His piercing black eyes and haughty air make me avoid confrontations with him whenever possible!"

Men Lamat chuckled. "Yes, I know how you feel, my dear. He does that on purpose. He has ways of making people feel helpless—an old priest's trick I will teach you to ignore. But how are you and Sak Ayi'in handling your day-to-day duties?"

"My sister and I—and our ladies-in-waiting—enjoy this busy palace life. People are always coming and going here. My schedule with the king includes my introductions to the nobility and their wives, and the priests and their families. It is always interesting to watch the weavers, painters, potters, and sculptors who are constantly in the palace—not to mention the jewelers who come to repair or fashion new polished jade, shell, or bone creations," she said with girlish enthusiasm.

"I have so many questions about Palenque, Uncle. I still don't feel completely comfortable asking the servants about my new home, even though the king's servant, Chan Och, a sweet old man, has offered to answer any of my questions. You are still my perfect teacher. For instance, there is constant talk of the drought that has overtaken the area, but more rain falls here in Palenque than in Tikal, don't you think?" Chanil poured her uncle a second cup of cacao and stirred it vigorously to make the foam rise on the top before she handed it to him.

"Yes, it is true, Chanil. And the residents take full advantage of the existing water supply. I marvel at how the water from the Cloud Center Valley—the *Tok-Tan*—flows into the Xocal Ha River and is then diverted to the aqueduct, which flows beneath the palace. It keeps a convenient and constant source of clean and flowing water for latrines and personal use and then flows to the irrigation troughs. It is truly wonderful how raised crop fields grow in what was once swampland. I see that besides corn, Palenque's farmers grow cacao, chilies, beans, and squash. No wonder we dine so well here!" he said, laughing. "Upon our arrival, I studied the fields and observed avocados, tobacco, cotton, and beets as well. Beekeepers keep beautiful gardens and guard their harmless little insects, which provide the palace with honey. The many fig trees here bear delicious fruit, and the bark from these trees supplies the paper on which the scribes detail Palenque's history.

"Have you noticed how water lilies grow in abundance in ponds and cultivated gardens around the palace, Chanil? Almost as important as the corn, these aquatic plants nourish the little fish we often eat. The farmers scatter the older water lily plants on top of the soil of the fields, where they decompose and nourish the earth below before planting season.

"But here I am, lecturing you as though you were a schoolgirl once again. It seems you are still burdened with me as your teacher, Chanil. However, Palenque is truly blessed, and even more so now that you have married the king!" Men Lamat laughed.

"My sweet Chanil, that brings me to the real reason I wanted to speak with you. Let us tour the garden near your room." As they walked the old scribe leaned in to speak in hushed tones. "How is your marriage to the king? I always prayed for a gentle husband for you and one who would treat you as a royal equal. The mother's lineage is very important here in Palenque, Chanil. They will want a child from your union, especially since you represent the royal lineage of Tikal. Think of your body as a pathway to the future of Palenque." The old man paused to choose his words carefully.

"King Akal has a daughter, Yax Koh, who is older than you are. I'm sure your new husband is aware of a young girl's insecurities and remembers to be gentle in his lovemaking to an inexperienced young woman such as you. If you must, put your mind elsewhere, but be certain the king is not aware of that. Make him feel as though you only think of him while he shares your bed.

"One last word of advice—if you are not ready to become a mother, make sure to use the combinations of herbs I taught you for … afterwards."

Chanil put a loving hand on the old man's arm. "Dear Uncle, you needn't worry. Akal is considerate and gentle, and I am grateful for all you have taught me. You have been both father and mother for most of my life. I truly would not have been able to understand a man—much less a king—without your thorough lessons. You may rest assured that I am a happily married woman. Now, let me walk back with you to your quarters."

The old priest knew how to read eyes as well as voices. Perhaps his niece believed her own words. Men Lamat still worried about the union he helped to create.

CHAPTER FIVE

On the return to her rooms, Chanil encountered a young man of about twenty-five *tuns* leaving Akal's throne room.

"Your Majesty," the young man said as he bowed low. "Welcome to Palenque. I am Cab Men Tun, King Akal's architect."

"Please arise and help me learn more about this beautiful palace, Cab Men Tun. I am fascinated with the architectural style, especially the unique arches supporting the ceilings." She looked up and around the hallway. "Why is the architecture here in Palenque different from that in Tikal?"

"Palenque's great architects decided the arches must be supported by strong lintels of mahogany crossbeams, giving each arch a flat top. I understand this is unique to Palenque, Your Majesty," he answered politely.

"I believe our painting style is also unique. Just as the palace exterior has flowers painted on its walls, so do the interior walls of the living quarters. This artwork is applied over solid backgrounds of red, green, purple, black, orange, or white. You may have noticed that some of the hallways showcase ceremonial scenes of bygone kings and queens. When painting the nobility, the painters' techniques are unusual in that they begin by intricately painting the sheer undergarments on Maya kings and their consorts. Each layer of clothing is then painted on top of the previous layer, as though the painters were carefully dressing the royal personages. I hope you and your beautiful sister are enjoying

Palenque's artwork and are happy here with your rooms and with the décor."

"Oh, we are, Cab Men Tun." Chanil smiled. "Everything is beautiful!"

"It is known all over the Maya lands that Palenque has limestone of exceptional quality, Your Majesty. The local limestone—the yellow precious *k'antuun*—is burned with seashells and sometimes snail shells to produce the fine powder that, when mixed with water, creates the paste used to paint over buildings and armatures of stone, resulting in the finest of walls and sculpture. Our skillfully carved wall panels are chiseled with flint tools and then meticulously sanded with soft stones so that the resulting work of art is so smooth, no chisel marks remain." The young man's pride in his city softened his large, dark eyes.

"I hope you have seen the beautiful work representing you and your status as queen, Your Majesty. Since your arrival, copious amounts of artwork have been created using the water lily symbol to represent your name. The water lily has been carved on building façades, and our scribes have drawn the lily symbol to describe your beauty and position in their codices—our archives, documenting the history of the Maya people of Palenque.

"Again, I hope you and your sister are happy here," the young architect said as he bowed.

It didn't escape her that the young man mentioned her sister twice to her in the conversation. "My sister and I are quite happy here, Cab Men Tun. I will tell Sak Ayi'in that you inquired about her well-being. Thank you for the history lesson as well." Chanil smiled at the thought of telling her sister about the architect who seemed interested.

Back in her rooms, Chanil appreciated the many sunlit windows allowing welcome breezes in through the finely woven and brightly embroidered curtains that danced in the wind. Lady Sak Ayi'in was waiting for Chanil there, admiring the mahogany shelves mounted on the walls to hold Chanil's hematite mirror on its stand and her pots of perfumed salves. Alongside them were her censers of the pine-scented copal, which her maids kept burning at night to ward off flying insects as she slept. Chanil took the statue of the goddess Ix Chel from the shelf and held it to her breast.

"We have much to be thankful for here in Palenque, Sak. I pray to Ix Chel each night in gratitude. Noblewomen and peasant women alike pray to the Lady Rainbow—our patron goddess of women's work, the nurse protector, midwife, and warrior. Our ceramic figurines and the palace glyphs portray the goddess as a very old, hook-nosed, and toothless woman, bent over with age—yet frighteningly powerful, isn't she?" Chanil stroked the ceramic figurine.

"But statues of her in her youth always show her as beautiful. I hope I don't become as homely in my old age, Chanil!" Lady Sak Ayi'in said. She walked to the queen's windows and looked out toward the city in wonderment. "It is even more breathtaking here than we were told. And I love the many breezy windows in this palace! I'm so glad these awnings of strong fabric bring much-needed shade to the several windows facing the glaring sun!"

"Yes, Sak. But I am particularly pleased with the queen's bath, which rests under a beautiful waterfall not too far from this end of the palace. I always make sure not to visit that delightful place if the First Wife and her adult daughter are there. Although courteous, neither woman has really welcomed me to Palenque. We have only seen one another at state ceremonies. Sak, I am so happy to have your company." The young queen took her sister's hand. They stood together in silence, taking in the view of the lush mountains.

"Mother would have been proud to see you here in this grand place—and married to a king of one of the four ruling cities. Do you think the palaces of Calakmul or Yaxchilán are as grand as this one? I don't think Tikal's is as beautiful," her sister said with a wistful glance in the direction of their home city so far away.

"I was just speaking to the king's young architect, Sak. He is very concerned that *you* like your life here. Have you met him yet?" Chanil probed.

"Oh, yes, he is very nice. I met him at your wedding. Yet I wonder what our life will be like here. Are you nervous about your future in this strange new city, Chanil?"

Smiling at her chatty, inquisitive sister, Queen Chanil gazed around deep in thought before answering. "I am living the life written in the stars for me before I was born, Sak Ayi'in. So although I am apprehensive about being a good wife and queen, I am grateful you and Uncle Men Lamat are here with me." She squeezed her sister's hand and hoped Lady Sak couldn't see the tears welling up in her dark eyes. She had no idea what the stars revealed of her fate.

CHAPTER SIX

The king's scribe, a young man of about twenty-five *tuns*, was assigned to be of service the new queen. Itz'At was slight of build, his long hair was tied back, and he wore little to no ornaments on his plain white tunic. It seemed he was always sitting cross-legged in a corner of the throne room with his bag of porcupine quills, paintbrushes, and pots of black ink while quietly working away on his codices. Itz'At became Chanil's confidant right away. She sought him out often during her first new moon cycle in Palenque. This quiet, unassuming young man was such a fixture at the palace, he was nearly invisible.

"I immediately felt comfortable turning to you for information about the various people who live or have business in the palace, Itz'At. Tell me about yourself and how you came to work for King Akal." Chanil gestured to the young servant to be seated in the garden near her rooms.

"Well, Your Majesty, my duties include chronicling important astronomical events, military campaigns, victories, and political decisions made by the king. I also take note of births, deaths, marriages, dynastic affairs, and palace propaganda, which I make sure are recorded into the bark paper codices. I also see to it that the best sculptors are then hired to translate the most important information onto carved temple walls and limestone tablets."

"But you appear to be so young, Itz'At," Chanil commented.

"If I may say so, Your Majesty, I had an artistic talent that showed itself at an early age, and my family knew I was born to be the scribe to the royal family. Being small of stature, I often felt intimidated by boys my age that played war games and rough sports. I was my happiest when imitating with a stick in the dirt the intricate characters I saw on the walls of the public buildings.

"After much sacrificing, bloodletting, and prayers to *Itzamná*—the highest god and patron of writing and the divinatory arts—my upper-class parents encouraged me to practice my glyphs and symbols tirelessly and to study under the king's aging scribe. My mother is a cousin to the First Wife, so I was welcomed into the palace. Under the king's scribe, I quickly learned which symbols imbued my texts with magical powers. My quiet nature also made me perfect for employment in the palace." Chanil could see he was a little uncomfortable speaking of his talents.

"By the time I was fifteen *tuns,* the old scribe died, and I was the natural replacement. My family and I prayed feverishly to the maize god—the original scribe, and also the first painter, dancer, and father to the revered Monkey Scribes. On the day I was presented to Ah Kan Mai, I was sworn to never reveal the secret magic rituals I would observe, and he instructed me that I must continue the tradition of recording only the palace events which showed the royal family and the priests in the best possible light. So I sit below the king's throne and record important decisions and visitations of emissaries and kings. I am privy to meetings even the nearly invisible fan-bearers cannot be present to observe."

"I have heard of your talent from the king, Itz'At," Queen Chanil said, smiling.

"I am only His Majesty's servant, my queen," the young scribe replied with a slight blush. "But I am told I create combinations of glyphs which are said to be understandable to all. I teach the pottery painters to repeat the most beautiful symbols on bowls, pitchers, vases, and incense pots. I enjoy training the sculptors to make only the most graceful symbols on the palace walls and sarcophagi, and I also oversee the painting of our murals for glyph and symbol accuracy, Your Majesty."

"Is the life of a worker in Palenque one of extreme hard labor as it is in Tikal, Itz'At? As a young niece of the king, I had more freedom there to explore the city for textiles and pottery, and so there I could observe the people more. Now I sometimes wish I could have a free moment to disguise myself and wander through the public areas away from the palace," Chanil revealed.

"Your Majesty, each time I venture into the city's shops for my paints and bark paper, I am reminded how alarming the dichotomy is between the lives of the peasants and the elite. For instance, the cacao bean is our currency and traded for goods in the marketplace. Peasants are paid one hundred cacao beans for a week's work—an amount that would only buy one rabbit or a turkey to feed a family for three or four days. One cacao bean pays for a lunchtime tomato or for a tamale sparsely filled with turkey, deer, or iguana meat. On the other hand, professionals connected with the palace, like myself, are paid forty thousand cacao beans every new moon cycle for a job well done."

"The cacao plants are plentiful in the highlands around Palenque, aren't they, Itz'At?" The queen was enjoying her chat with her intelligent new friend.

"Yes, Your Majesty—as long as the spider monkeys that love to feast on the cacao pods are kept in check!" They both laughed.

"But what about the people of Palenque?" asked Chanil. She missed her familiar life in Tikal and was hungry to know more about her new city.

"Peasant men toil in the fields, at construction, or as artisans. Their wives and daughters kneel on the earth to grind the dried cacao beans on stone *metates,* just as they grind the dried corn for the cornmeal flour. Their clay tortilla griddles, which are easily made in great quantities, are traded for a woven basket or mat or spools of colored cotton.

"Peasant women, as well as women in the elite households, do the weaving for their families' clothing," the scribe continued. "From small family plots of land, they collect the cotton fibers and weave them into necessary clothing and household items on their back-strap looms—those simple devices made from horizontal sticks bound to a frame of vertical ones and tied by a rope to the weaver's waist. Their own beautiful family patterns are woven between the sticks."

"Yes, Itz'At," Queen Chanil agreed, "I too work on my back-strap loom. It gives me such peace to create fabric with my favorite colored threads."

"I see women weaving everywhere they gather—indoors or outside—as they tend to children. Although the women of the royal household have beautifully carved and personalized tools like bone picks and weaving needles such as you may have, the simple peasant women use more basic wooden tools. Yet they still create exquisite textiles of magnificent colors as beautiful as any bird of the forest. These fine fabrics of Palenque are traded to other cities and are well-known throughout the Mayan Empire.

"As I stroll the narrow walkways between vendors' stalls, I admire the old women sitting cross-legged, weaving elaborate mats for sleeping or the fine baskets traded for other goods. Their beautiful woven palm fiber bases for noblemen's headdresses are lightweight, yet strong and finely crafted to allow the attachment of hundreds of feathers and shells or colorful fabrics."

"The pottery here in Palenque far surpasses ours in Tikal," Queen Chanil said. "Some of the women pottery painters are teaching me to paint on a few pieces. I am fascinated watching them and trying my hand at creating accurate calligraphic designs myself. It brings me joy to learn something new."

"I would be happy to assist you with your pottery pieces any time you ask, Your Majesty. The peasant women make basic pottery by collecting clay from the riverbank, mixing it with sand and ash, and then rolling it into coils," Itz 'At explained. "The coiled clay is worked and smoothed to form a tall cylinder, a vase, or a wide bowl. The object is then smoothed to a fine finish and baked. When the pottery is done, it is ready for the palace's fine artists … like yourself." He grinned. "As you know, on top of the cream background color, they use black and red pigments to paint detailed, lifelike scenes of court activities or scenes from tales of the ancient gods. They bake the piece once more, and the work of art is completed.

"I have taken note of your skill at weaving and calligraphy, Your Highness," Itz'At said. Her simple but superb handiwork adorned the king's favorite capes. The servants also whispered that she often happily worked alongside the cooks who prepared the king's meals. Seeing the queen in the kitchen was an unusual sight, and it took the cooks and servants some time to adjust to her presence and laugh with her as though she were one of them.

"But what about the children of Palenque, Itz'At?" Queen Chanil said. "I worry about them. It is evident that many of the children of peasant families are smaller and sickly."

"They eat meager meals of cooked corn, beans, squash, and an occasional meat stew, Your Majesty. Upper-class women have servants who cook fine meals containing a variety of vegetables and meats like turkey, deer, rabbit, and fish for healthy and well-fed children. Although our city is beautiful, our children are hungry."

"Let us see if together we can help in some way, Itz'At. Thank you for the education about my new city," the queen said, turning toward her rooms.

The young scribe had great respect for Lady Chanil. In spite of the queen's youth, she was learning her duties well and was loved by the household of servants. Little did she know how treacherous palace life in Palenque could be.

CHAPTER SEVEN

AD 871

"The people must be appeased." The high priest spoke softly to his minions as they approached the king's throne room. "It seems that since the new queen arrived, there is an obvious restlessness in the people of Palenque. I have called for an audience with the king. The only way this intrusion of the young queen can be controlled is if she gives birth to a young prince whom we would then mold into the monarch Palenque needs. According to our calendar, which tracks solar, lunar, and local time, the opportunity for conception is perfect now."

When advised by servants to enter, the three under-priests prostrated themselves on the floor, and Ah Kan Mai bowed from his waist in greeting. King Akal sat cross-legged on a carved stone throne covered in jaguar skin pillows. His fan-bearers stood on either side of him. The high priest stepped forward and began his careful request.

"Oh Great *Ahau*, King of Kings, descended from the sun!" Ah Kan Mai proclaimed, bowing low. "We know you remember the failed peasant uprising just two *tuns* past. To prevent another rebellion and to appease the people, we dare ask you and your bride, Queen Chanil Nab Chel, to bring forth an heir to the throne—a First Sprout who will renew the people's pride in their king. The planet Venus is in alignment for his conception at the full moon, predicted in two nights. We pray to the gods you are blessed with a *ba'ah ch'ok* before this *tun* is over." Ah Kan Mai bowed low. "Although you are over forty *tuns* older than Queen Chanil, may we remind you that the great Bird Jaguar of Cozumel fathered a son at the age of sixty *tuns* with his consort, Great-Skull-Zero. If it pleases the king, it has been read in the planets that a son could be conceived at this time."

"Prepare the palace for a prayer ceremony in two nights, Ah Kan Mai," ordered Lord Akal. "Our great city and its people deserve an heir." His thoughts settled on his barren daughter for an instant, but immediately traveled to his beautiful new wife, and he smiled. "A First Sprout is what we all need!"

On the evening of the full moon, Queen Chanil had her arms, back, and upper chest painted with her favorite mixture of the pulp from the red axiote pods, fine clay, lime ashes, and the ground-up insects that feed on the cactus. Over the reddish-brown base on the queen's shoulders, cheeks, and chest, her lady-in-waiting painted holy symbols representing fertility and childbirth in light hues of blue and yellow. This artfully applied body paint not only brought attention to Chanil's beautiful shoulders and long arms, but also served to protect her delicate white skin from the ever-present biting insects attracted to the lights of the torches.

Just as the sun set, the king and Chanil, flanked by six priests, walked in a solemn procession to the Great Temple. The king took her hand as they stood tall and straight in their cumbersome ceremonial garb of heavy, brightly colored woven capes and collars, tall headdresses, and elaborate jewelry. As royal custom dictated, they carefully and regally climbed the steep steps of the temple. With great effort Chanil, maneuvered her heavy robe of state without looking down or losing her balance until she reached the top with Akal.

Chanil felt the magic of the night as the priests chanted and the sweet and pungent copal censers burned. She stood on the platform of the pyramid that contained the remains of at least seven kings who had once ruled over the great city. Chanil looked to her left at the wall carving of an earlier Palenque queen holding a child, and she understood why this temple was the perfect place for such a ceremony. Ah Kan Mai handed the king's two assistants the specially carved gourd which held the hallucinogenic potion the king would insert for his ritual enema.

"Oh, Great K'awiil," implored King Akal as he entered the trance state. "Divine patron of the great Maya lineage and the essence of fertility, we appeal to you as we burn the precious copal and send you our prayers. As you have blessed Palenque with fertile earth, may our great city be blessed with a *ba'ah ch'ok* through the union of your two servants before you."

Akal sat cross-legged on his throne, and using the holy K'awiil perforator, carefully pierced the skin under his phallus, thus allowing him to participate in divine procreation. The perforator was carved in the shape of the god K'awiil, with his customary torch-shaped head and snake face, and made from the holy flint sent by K'awiil in a lightning strike. The handle was shaped like a single serpent tail. After his piercing, Akal offered his blood on fig bark paper to the priests.

Chanil pierced her tongue and prayed, "Oh great and beneficent Ix Chel, goddess of childbirth, rainbows, and the moon, wife of our great god Itzamná, bless the sacred seed of your son, Lord Akal Balam, this night. As I am named for the water lily, the fertile flower of the earth, I pray that when the king's *k'awiil* is planted in my womb, his seeds germinate and grow as the sacred corn plant grows in the fertile fields of Palenque. And as the corn nourishes us, may our offspring nourish the greatness of the Maya people in reverence to you."

Chanil handed her blood-soaked papers to the priests for burning.

"Ba'ah ch'ok k'uhul ba'akah ahau," the priests chanted as they put fire to the precious offering mixed with the sweet copal incense and prayed to the gods for a young heir to be the next sacred lord of Palenque.

Alone in the king's chambers, Akal gently spoke to his new queen. "You truly light up my life, as the rainbow graces the sky after a dark storm."

She was like a narcotic to him, much like the one derived from the water lily, a fitting flower that was a part of her name. With her, he felt young again, and once more the strong leader his people believed him to be. His first wife, Lady Zac Ku, was as old as he was now. Their daughter had married a nobleman of weak character and even weaker health. Palenque would fall to Lady Zac Ku's greedy brother if anything should happen to the king. He was right to choose a Second Wife from the city of Tikal. The thought of siring an heir to the throne with this woman made him desire Chanil Nab Chel even more, his body remembering the lust of youth once again. Tikal's greatest treasure lay in his arms, and he would take what was his.

CHAPTER EIGHT

The news Ah Kan Mai had been waiting for was finally announced. The queen's uncle, Men Lamat, determined that Lady Chanil Nab Chel was with child. For two full moons, she had missed her monthly blood flows and was expected to give birth 260 days from the time of conception—just as the sacred corn was planted on this rotation. It was time for the high priest's plan to begin.

Ah Kan Mai sought out the massive slave from the priests' quarters where he had been housing him and having him perform menial labor. "Your life is about to change once more, Chukah. I am recommending to the king that you be placed in the queen's private quarters. If the king chooses to trust you there, you will have a life that is much better than any of your family or class. However, if you displease the king in any way, it will reflect on me, and consequently, you will be quite an impressive sacrifice for the gods." They paused in the hall outside the king's chambers. "One more thing, Chukah." The high priest's eyes bore into the big man's face. "Always remember that *I* am your ultimate superior. Stay here until I call for you."

Chan Och greeted them outside of the king's chambers. The king's old servant hardly masked his surprise at the giant who stood behind the high priest. "Greetings, Ah Kan Mai. The king is aware you wished to see him. Follow me." He accompanied the high priest to where King Akal sat at his desk.

"Well, Ah Kan Mai, I have been curious about the important introduction you have for me since you mentioned it this morning in the throne room."

"Your Majesty, I know you must now fear for the safety of your new wife and the child in her womb," Ah Kan Mai began, bowing low. "May I suggest that the slave I brought to the palace, Chukah Nuk T'zi, would be the ideal bodyguard and chief attendant for the new queen? I found him in the limestone quarries, and because of his enormous size, I felt he would be better suited as an attendant to your new wife. This giant slave is no ordinary peasant. He has been assisting me in menial tasks, but I feel he would be a formidable guard for the young queen.

"If you don't care to give him a place in the family's quarters, I can always put him to work elsewhere or just send him back to the quarries. He appears mute, but since his intelligence is evident, his silence should be of no concern to you, Great Ahau."

"Yes, I have heard of him from the servants, but have yet to meet him. Chan Och, please bring the man in here so I may see this giant for myself." The king's expression turned from curiosity to interest as the old man brought the slave before him. Akal studied the huge man's face and then walked around him, as if assessing a piece of furniture brought to him as a war treasure.

"His name is Chukah Nuk T'zi, Great Ahau."

"Ah Kan Mai, as long as he takes orders, tends to the queen's every whim, and would always be present to guard my infant son, I accept him," King Akal said. "I will introduce him to his queen. Thank you, Ah Kan Mai. I know I can always trust your judgment. Now, come with me, Chukah."

The high priest smiled as he bowed and gave the giant one last piercing glare as a reminder of his earlier command before he left the king's quarters. *My emissary is now conveniently placed in the heart of the king's chambers.*

"This is where I expect you to spend your days, Chukah," King Akal said as he gestured to the hall outside the queen's quarters. "You have a good view of the royal family's private hallways. Mostly women mill about in this vicinity, with the First Wife's rooms there, and the new queen's rooms here, and mine in between. I'll wager this view is much more pleasurable here than the limestone quarries," the king said with a laugh. "I'll return for you momentarily."

Akal found Chanil sitting in front of a breezy window. It was a drizzly, humid, and hot afternoon. She was attempting to find some cool comfort for her changing body when the king entered.

"Chanil, I have a slave I would like to present to you. I know when you see him, you'll understand why I would like him to be your new guard."

"Of course, Akal. Please bring him here."

The king returned quickly, accompanied by a giant man who stood three heads taller than her husband. "Chanil, this is Chukah Nuk T'zi. He looks fearful, but he is sworn to protect you. With him here, I know I will feel better about your safety when I am away."

Queen Chanil gazed curiously at the huge man and smiled as she placed a protective hand on her womb. Palace gossip had preceded his appearance, but Chanil was nonetheless surprised at the man's size. He looked at the floor in respect to her status as she spoke. "The king's son and I are grateful for your protection, Chukah." The enormous slave respectfully bowed.

"He cannot speak, Chanil, but he understands all commands. I have shown him where he will stand in the hallway just outside your rooms," the king assured her.

"In that case, I already feel safer," Chanil said comfortably as she reached for her husband's hand. "I'm afraid your work here outside my door will be quite boring, Chukah. I am glad you are here, yet I hope your strength never has to be tested." Chukah bowed again and began his new life as he took his place at attention outside the queen's doorway.

CHAPTER NINE

Toward the end of the month of *Zotz,* the time of the planting, Chanil felt her first pains. After one long, excruciating day of labor, the concerned midwives gave her a hot tea of honey and salt, and the priests began their prayers to the goddess Ix Chel, the patron god of childbirth.

Men Lamat took charge as Chanil's sister, and the roomful of women began to look worried.

"Place hot stones on the queen's abdomen to ease the pains," he ordered the servants. "Lady Sak Ayi'in, it is time to pierce your tongue and offer a blood sacrifice and fervent prayers to Ix Chel. She aids women suffering from a difficult childbirth."

The old priest stood near Chanil's bedside and stroked her hair as he did when she had a fever as a child. "Chanil, I promise you, your mother suffered a long labor giving birth to you, so this is not unusual. Rest assured that all predictions are for a healthy boy for you and King Akal," the old priest said softly as he patted Chanil's hand. He bowed and left the room, promising to be nearby.

Men Lamat walked to where the giant, Chukah Nuk T'zi, stood outside of the queen's chambers. "Chukah, it seems that after today, your duties increase. The queen will need your protection even more, as will her son, who will be born soon. I know you hear me, I am aware you cannot speak; yet I see true intelligence in your eyes and a deep sense of responsibility to your queen. We are all fortunate to have you here in the palace. Never be afraid to use your own judgment in defending the queen or her family. Wherever you have come from, I believe the gods have sent you here. Thank you, Chukah."

Lady Sak held her sister's hand, happy for the moment. "In spite of the agony I see you are experiencing, Chanil, I still envy you."

"It is almost nightfall, Sak. I am exhausted but relieved, because these more frequent and intense pains signal the time for Palenque's heir to take his place in the world," Chanil whispered through her frequent deep breaths. "Sak … it is time!" was all Queen Chanil could manage to gasp before the urge to push overwhelmed her.

"Wrap her now!" Sak Ayi'in commanded.

Chanil's attendants stood on either side of the platform which supported her sleeping pallet. They swiftly wrapped her belly and hips with the long birthing sash and pulled it taut with each contraction. Chanil reached above her to the cords which hung from the ceiling rafters and pushed down with all her might. Exhausted as she was, her strength held, and finally her son was born.

Lady Sak saw that the infant was surely a royal Maya, as evidenced by his long limbs and fair complexion. She held the beautiful baby boy for her sister to see. "He is perfect, Chanil," Sak Ayi'in said in awe above loud hollers from the pink infant. "Prepare him for his mother," she urged the servants over their happy clucking of tongues. The attendants rushed to touch him and clean his fair skin.

Muluc wrapped the little *unen* in the finest cotton cloths and presented the baby boy to his tired but happy mother. "Your Majesty, it is such a privilege for the other servants and myself to be present at the little prince's birth," Muluc said.

"I am happy you are here, too, Muluc. I needed all the help you and the others offered me."

Lady Sak and the servants could see the special love in their queen's eyes as she held her newborn son and began to learn his body and sounds. It was not often one was so fortunate as to witness a royal birth.

"Muluc, bring Men Lamat to her now," Lady Sak said. "Our uncle will surely be pleased, Chanil. The goddess has heard our prayers."

Within a few minutes, Men Lamat approached the queen and her baby son. "You have performed your royal duty to perfection, my dear," he whispered, tucking the baby's blanket securely. "I see your mother in this child's face, and I feel your father's strong hands as the boy grips my fingers. Now I hope you can rest," he said as he kissed her hand. "Lady Sak, come with me to announce the birth to the king."

Ah Kan Mai approached Queen Chanil's private chambers and watched Men Lamat and the queen's sister enter the king's quarters. The giant stood there at attention, guarding the doorway.

"Don't get too comfortable with your accommodations, Dog. I may have need of your assistance soon," the high priest muttered as he entered the queen's rooms.

Chanil's ladies-in-waiting were washing her. He relished their angry stares. Watching intently, Ah Kan Mai explained, "I must examine the infant for the greenish-color spot at his sacral region. I will determine if he is indeed of royal blood, Your Majesty."

The high priest took the baby from Chanil and turned the infant over as if the child was an animal being inspected. Ah Kan Mai found what he was looking for at the base of the baby's spine and proclaimed, "This child is a true Maya! His predetermined name is K'in Balam. May he have the wisdom of a prophet and the blessings of our Jaguar god, Lord of the Jungle!" He handed the new little prince back to Chanil. *Was that repulsion in her eyes? Well, her belly* was *exposed to my sight as the midwife wrapped her tightly.* Ah Kan Mai bowed and smiled before he departed.

Besides the dark green sacral spot, the high priest noticed how fair the baby's skin was. It was obvious his arms and legs were exceptionally long and lean—a second indication the newborn was truly a royal Maya offspring who would grow to tower over the people. Ah Kan Mai had only seen one other such baby in Piedras Negras many *tuns* past, but the child hadn't lived past infancy.

As the priest headed toward his rooms, his thoughts raced. *There are so few real Mayas left. The kings have too often mixed the royal blood with the squat-bodied peasantry and even with Mexican blood. Now that the young queen has bred a king, I will have to carefully plan how I will control the king and this interfering new wife.*

Her baby boy nursed hungrily at her breast, and happiness replaced Chanil's anger at the high priest's intrusion. K'in Balam had thick black hair and long, tiny fingers and toes. Looking at his innocent face, she found it difficult to imagine how this helpless infant would one day rule a great people.

As her son suckled, Chanil thought about daily life and realized her sister and ladies-in-waiting were the only women who influenced her. But Chanil often found them tiresome and their conversation uninteresting. The king's description of his duties and the politics existing between Palenque and its vassals was so much more appealing. The only real father she could remember was Uncle Men Lamat. His pride in her and his kind encouragement had made her want to succeed in any endeavor. Her husband, uncle, and new little son were the only men who mattered to her now.

A gentle cough interrupted her thoughts. "Have you recovered from the ordeal of childbirth, my love?" The king timidly entered her bedroom and stroked the soft cheek of his sleeping son. "Our boy is handsome and indeed perfect. I cannot imagine being more proud."

"It is good to have a quiet moment with our little one and you, Akal," Chanil answered, beginning to feel the effects of the chaya tea she was given to calm her and prevent anemia. "I wish my mother and father were alive to see this miracle that carries their blood, as well as that of a great king. I can almost envision my beautiful mother's soft cooing to her first grandson and my father's brusque approval. It seems so very long ago that I last gazed upon their faces. Now their funerals are my most vivid memories of them."

"Your parents would have been proud of you and this precious boy. Thank you for giving birth to our son, Chanil. You know, I was born at the beginning of this *baktun*. As you may remember from your studies, this 384-*tun* period is predicted to be the start of the fall of our great Maya race. Perhaps you have given us a new beginning. The royal household will soon celebrate our son's birth with the people. I will leave you to your happy dreams now."

Chanil had barely fallen asleep when, too soon, the parade of priests entered the room with a clacking of shells and clutching bowls of smoking incense to bless K'in Balam. They placed a bone in the special *lac* of pure rainwater specifically caught in a cacao tree. Touching it to his forehead and between his tiny fingers and toes, they pronounced his birthday auspicious. Then they took him away to the ceremonial plaza to join the royal household. During that time, Chanil was taken to her steam bath, where she sat welcoming the silence and privacy her personal *pib nah* offered.

Muluc poured hot water over the hissing hot rocks and then picked up a soft cloth to wash Chanil's body. She explained what the other servants told her would happen. "The king, the priests, and even the First Wife are all gathered before the thousands of waiting people who have thronged in the main plaza for their first glimpse of the future king. The royal family will perform the bloodletting ceremony in honor of the newborn. Then they will anoint a bowl of holy corn with the baby's blood from his umbilical cord. That corn will be quite holy when it is planted! Then they will burn the afterbirth and announce to the cheering people K'in Balam's place in succession to the throne of Palenque. It is all so exciting, Your Majesty!"

"I am too exhausted to care much for all the ceremonies. I just want to go back and hold little K'in Balam," Chanil said with a yawn.

Back in her room, Chanil waited for her beautiful baby. But she was only allowed a few more precious moments with her son before K'in Balam was delivered to the nursemaids. She wanted to hold him a while longer after his second feeding, but palace customs were stronger than her exhausted arguments.

The queen took one last look at his little round head before K'in Balam was taken to his crib. There the nurses would strap his head in a slanted wooden frame. As he slept, it would ensure the perfect shaping of his royal Maya skull.

CHAPTER TEN

I t had been two days since the birth of Akal's baby son. Lady Zac Ku frowned upon realizing she was growing weary of the weight of being queen and First Wife. Still, the intruder's title as Second Wife disturbed and unsettled her. Although Akal ascended the throne only ten *tuns* past, the royal rituals were taking their toll on Lady Zac Ku. She was reaching the end of her life and had to finally face her greatest fears. Not only was her body disappointing her with its pains and crippled joints, but her husband of thirty-five *tuns* was also a different person since his new marriage.

She couldn't blame him for wanting to marry a beautiful young woman—although he had assured her it was to avoid a war with Tikal. She saw with sadness how he had become almost indifferent to her. Now, with a new son from the Woman of Tikal, the old queen's fear over her daughter's dwindling claim to the throne had become a grim reality.

Lady Zac Ku knew how age had changed her. In her youth, she had been trim, but a certain plumpness was expected due to her maturity and status. She did not appreciate the matronly representations of her on palace walls, yet she was proud of her life of leisure and good food. Although the people professed to love her, she knew she was being unfavorably compared to the new Second Wife. She also knew that "plump, short, and crippled" was how the citizens of Palenque perceived her.

Her daughter, Lady Yax Koh, was a much younger mirror image of her mother—short of stature with a square torso. Although Yax Koh had the same body type as the peasants, she could not conceive as easily as they did. Still, she had hopes of producing a child at the late age of thirty-five *tuns*. Lady Zac Ku watched her daughter hungrily eating a plateful of after-dinner sweets in the old queen's chambers.

"I think my father loves his new baby son more than he loves me!" Lady Yax Koh wailed. "He practically ignores me, Mother. Is it because I cannot give him the grandchild he has waited for—the precious heir he wanted? I hate her!" she sobbed, taking another mouthful.

"Calm down, Yax Koh," the old queen snapped impatiently. "Crying won't get him to visit you."

"For ten *tuns,* the priests have prescribed potions and performed bloodletting ceremonies for me and my husband," whined Yax Koh. "We have endured countless Bundle Rites. I have buried cloth bundles of sacred beads, shells, and sky stones—all to ensure a successful conception. Even my wearing precious blue-green jade jewelry—the color of fertility—does not bring the magic of new life to my belly. I am constantly being reminded the matrilineal line is important to the Maya people, and still I continue struggling to conceive, especially now that there is an intruder who would take our royal ancestry and end it with the blood of the noble families of Tikal! Mother, I don't know what else to do!"

"Believe me, I am weary of defending you to my brother, Yahan K'ahk, who expects to step in as king of Palenque if anything were to happen to Akal. But don't give up just yet, my daughter. Go and lay with your husband. I will speak with someone who may help."

Perhaps it was in the stars that Palenque's future was with the child of an outsider. But before she gave in completely, Lady Zac Ku decided to speak with the one person whom she knew hated the intruder—Ah Kan Mai.

The high priest had known she would come, but he was surprised at how long it had taken for the old queen to finally seek him out. Ah Kan

Mai was in his observatory this quiet warm night, studying the heavens for a way to rid the palace of the young woman who held his king besotted. He had determined that the time of the solar eclipse would be a perfect opportunity for an "accident" to happen to the new wife or her baby son. He and his new conspirator had exactly three moons to arrange it. Except for the two of them, no one would know the plan.

Ah Kan Mai was well aware that Lady Zac Ku was not an educated woman and had found ways to avoid her lessons as a young girl while being groomed for aristocracy. Her father had been a much-respected *sahal* whose political opinion was sought by many. Having lived near the palace as a girl, she was obviously a good student of character. She had been fascinated watching her aunt, Palenque's last queen, rule with unforgiving fervor. The high priest knew Lady Zac Ku had never liked him, but he knew she needed him now.

"Welcome to my piece of the palace, Lady Zac Ku." Ah Kan Mai smiled in greeting. The old queen had struggled to make it up the four stories to his room high above the royal buildings and was huffing too hard to speak. He offered her a stool to sit on, but she waved him away with her gnarled hand and long, claw-like fingernails.

"Please, let me see the world as you do, for a moment," she gasped, catching her breath. "The view of the palace grounds below intrigues me far more than the expanse of the heavens, which interests you." She leaned against the tower window and looked down. "Ah! The moonlight illuminates the inner courtyards and the passage to the baths. I marvel at the incredible view of the fertile valleys of Palenque. No wonder you are always in this tower. You can spy on everyone below!" Lady Zac Ku laughed. "I'll have to remember that."

"It is a pity the night sky obscures a better observation of the world below, My Lady, for if it were a clear day, you could see the ocean to the north. Perhaps you will grant me many more visits, My Queen."

"I doubt I would survive another journey up those steps. For our next meeting, you will come to me." She spoke clearly, with no further trace of exhaustion.

"What has brought you here this late at night and at such stress to your body?" Ah Kan Mai asked, concealing his excitement by looking intently at the stars.

"I am sure you already know. You can stop the dramatics for my benefit," the queen answered, deciding to sit on the stool after all. "My daughter's future brings me here. I don't expect she'll give Akal a grandson at this point, but I also don't want her cast out of the palace after I am gone. What do you see in our future?"

Choosing not to tell her—or anyone, for that matter—about the coming eclipse, he spoke in a vague manner. "As you know, we say, 'as above, so below.' I have seen in the stars that a great and sad event will occur here in the palace within three *uinals*. I do not yet know what is going to happen, but my sense is that it has something to do with the new queen or her son."

"What about that giant who guards her door? He isn't about to let harm come to the young woman," Lady Zac Ku said. "In fact, wouldn't the giant be a particularly special gift in sacrifice to the gods? I imagine Palenque would be doubly blessed by such an offering."

"I wouldn't worry about the slave; I brought him here, and he has my allegiance," Ah Kan Mai assured, then subtly changed the subject. "Have you heard that two more children from the valley have died of the bite of the deadly *nauyaca?* Aren't we fortunate that we have such dedicated servants in the palace who rid our rooms of the pit vipers from the cornfields?"

"Ah Kan Mai, I understand what you are saying, and I have decided you are a poor liar and much too obvious." Rising to leave, she smiled broadly, showing the polished jade beads inset in the center of each front tooth.

"Yes, I have heard about those poor children, but the workers are so prolific, they'll have replaced their little ones before the next planting season. My old bones just want my *t'zite* tea and to go to bed now. But before I do, perhaps I'll use some *t'zite* beans to create a spell of my own. When you have decided on a plan, let me know how I may assist—for the sake of my daughter and the future of Palenque." Lady Zac Ku heaved her body up and pushed away his outstretched arm.

❧

Ah Kan Mai watched her lumber across the courtyard below. He knew his strategy to get rid of Queen Chanil Nab Chel would take careful planning and a little patience. The eclipse would be very soon. A helpless infant could be whisked into oblivion in an instant. Getting rid of a strong young woman would be a challenge, but with a giant and an old queen as allies in the innermost rooms of the palace, it was not an impossible task.

CHAPTER ELEVEN

Lady Zac Ku walked to Chanil's rooms. It was late, but with an infant to care for, the young mother would not yet be asleep. As the older queen approached the massive guard, he merely bowed and let her pass. She regally brushed past the young female servant who looked surprised and then afraid, but gestured her into Chanil's rooms. Upon entering, Lady Zac Ku paused, taken aback by the absolute beauty of the new mother as she nursed Palenque's heir. Fighting her own maternal instincts toward the young woman, she approached Chanil and interrupted the peaceful moment.

"You must be proud to have given the king the son he has wanted for many *tuns,* Lady Chanil. I see how powerfully he nurses at your breast. He is a healthy boy."

"Thank you, Lady Zac Ku. I am honored you have come to pay your respects. May I have Muluc bring you refreshment?"

"No, thank you. I am about to retire for the night, but I felt the need to speak to you before doing so. The time is late, and I will not bother you with idle conversation. I hope you understand the king has a daughter who may well bear a son to ascend the throne of Palenque. It is important to our people that the Palenque lineage is not broken. Perhaps the same is true in Tikal—your home." Lady Zac Ku heard the bitterness in her own voice. "I am sorry I have not welcomed you properly to Palenque. When you are up and about, we will have to sit down with a strong cup of cacao and get to know one another a little better." She forced a smile, hoping she didn't look as old and unattractive as she felt.

"I would be happy to have the opportunity to talk with you and perhaps your daughter as well. Thank you for your visit." Chanil fought a yawn as the nursemaid came to put the baby to bed.

"Until our next visit, then." Lady Zac Ku tilted her head and turned to walk away without limping, no matter how painful her hips were. *I wonder what Ah Kan Mai has in mind? I'm sure my brother will be happy to aid in any plan which will allow our life to return to what it once was,* she thought as she crossed the hallway to her rooms. Yet in her heart, she knew that since the arrival of Queen Chanil, nothing would ever be the same.

CHAPTER TWELVE

The next morning, Akal sat alone in his throne room. He contemplated his life, his beautiful new wife, and the precious son she had given him. He also pondered the possibility of another war to appease his hungry and growing middle class. After smoking his strong cigar, Palenque's king studied his treasured mirror for its portents. This *nehn* was a gift from the king of Tikal upon Akal's marriage to Chanil. A carved wooden figure of a dwarf held the mirror, set in a turtle shell, at the perfect angle for the king to see himself in its reflection.

"Your baby son is indeed a gift of the gods, Akal." Lady Zac Ku spoke softly as she approached her husband. "Why am I feeling that after thirty-five *tuns,* we have almost become strangers? Still, I am happy your wish for a son has finally come to pass."

"Yes, he is a marvel. But we have had a fine life together, Zac Ku. Our daughter may yet honor us with a grandchild to carry on your family's royal bloodline."

"Maybe not, Akal. But in the future, I hope you will not forget our many *tuns* as husband and wife and the happy moments with your daughter. Even though she is a grown woman, Yax Koh still seeks your guidance and expects you to visit with her every now and then."

Reminded that his daughter was a simple and unattractive woman, the king felt a pang of guilt, knowing his fatherly duties were lacking where she was concerned. Akal had to admit to himself that he had never gotten over wanting a son. His happiest memories of Yax Koh were when she was a sweet little girl. But as she became a woman, Akal saw his wife too clearly in her, and he found them both difficult to understand. Grateful for the noisy interruption of the visiting lords bringing their cities' tributes, the king motioned for Lady Zac Ku to be seated in her place under the draperies behind and to the left of his throne.

While Akal accepted the gifts of precious goods from the vassal cities, his thoughts were on his new son. K'in Balam was proving to be the Little Sprout he had been nicknamed. The baby suckled voraciously, smiled readily, and soon became the reason for his father's very existence. Akal's daily visits to Chanil's rooms had become more frequent, because being with his new wife and son was the highlight of his day. Dealing with aristocrats squabbling over land, slaves, and farms; keeping up the morale up of his troops; and attending the sacrifices of enemy captives were becoming less and less a priority. He began to leave more of these duties to Ah Kan Mai, who sat near the king as usual. Akal noted absently that the high priest seemed more short-tempered and impatient of late.

"Ah Kan Mai, have these bundles of shells, salt, and cacao beans tallied. I have a more important task!" He stood and headed for Chanil's rooms. There he held his baby son in his arms, and was once again aware of how fragile and helpless the little one would be without his protection.

"Chukah Nuk T'zi!" He called out for the servant standing at attention outside his wife's rooms. The giant entered and bowed. "I expect you to make it your life's duty to protect my wife and son whenever I am not here," the king declared. "The moment harm comes to either one of them is the moment your life ends. Am I understood?"

Chukah's slight bow of his huge head was the only acknowledgement the king needed. Looking up at the giant, Akal merely had to think the words, *Thank you.* The men understood one another. The king had no idea the servant's promise would soon be tested.

CHAPTER THIRTEEN

The day of the eclipse had finally arrived. Ah Kan Mai knew the time to act was at hand. The watchful priest had seen the king's distracted expression the day before as he gave his orders to handle the king's duties. He saw the old queen's anger, too. Ah Kan Mai was more certain than ever he must act soon.

The previous night, the priest had had another disturbing dream: in this one the king's new son's umbilicus had become two intertwined snakes, connecting him to the gods. They hissed and rattled their tails upon seeing Ah Kan Mai and broke free to chase and attempt to strangle him.

He awoke in a sweat and vowed something had to be done immediately. Perhaps the snakes in his dream were the inspiration he needed. Ah Kan Mai paced his room nervously as he planned the day.

The high priest would take a servant with him that morning to the *cols*—the closest cornfields—and find a *nauyaca* to bring back to the palace. In all the confusion of the eclipse and ensuing darkness, he would have a few precious seconds to release the snake from its basket into baby K'in Balam's crib. With luck, Queen Chanil would pick up her crying baby and also receive a deadly bite. If not, Ah Kan Mai would be sure to console the grief-stricken king with drink and drugs. He would convince Akal the baby's death was the fault of the young queen. How the king chose to punish her would be directly related to how drugged he would be.

Where is that stupid servant? I'll tell him we are going to look for herbs for my potions, and if he is obedient, I will teach him how to prepare an elixir to give his lover.

With a giddy laugh, Ah Kan Mai began to imagine the power he would have over the king and the old queen—he power he had begun to savor before that woman of Tikal had ruined his plans. Ah Kan Mai enjoyed his private meetings with King Akal and the assurance he had the king's ear. At last, he heard sandals quickly approaching his room.

"You're late! If you are late again, I will personally pull out each of your fingernails!" the priest exploded as the nervous young servant of fifteen *tuns* cowered in a corner. "Now pick up that basket and follow me out to the valley. We will be searching the cornfields for special herbs."

The day was dark and cloudy. Ah Kan Mai worried the black clouds would obscure the eclipse which figured so prominently in his plans. He had made a special proclamation to the people the week before, warning them the gods had been displeased and their anger might result in a tragedy. If the palace inhabitants couldn't see the eclipse, they would go on about their day as usual.

He needed them to be fearful and preoccupied with the abnormal midday darkness. It was a pity the queen had already given birth. If a pregnant woman gazed at the *chibil chin*—the "sun's bite"—the baby would automatically be born defective. Little K'in Balam appeared very healthy now, but the priest would make sure it would not be for long.

Ah Kan Mai was pleased that heavy mists coated the entire vicinity beneath the palace. He wore an uncommonly plain tunic and no headdress. Although he wore his usual large, carved jade pectoral pendants, he looked more like a *sahal* on official business than the high priest of Palenque. The journey down the steps from the palace complex to the valley below was a dismal experience. The servant, Ah Tok, a sniveling boy, whimpered and mumbled until they reached the raised cornfields just beginning to show young heads of the precious corn.

As they strode up and down, Ah Tok searched for a mysterious herb while Ah Kan Mai's dark almond eyes scanned the cornfield for the dreaded *nauyaca,* knowing these deadly snakes hid themselves well in the soil and leaves. They were almost invisible to even the most practiced eye. The priest searched for the familiar triangular head and row of pyramid-shaped markings down the length of the snake's tan and brown-scaled body. *Ah! There!* He finally spotted a huge, curled-up specimen napping between meals and nearly hidden under the dead corn leaves. *This one would most surely be the length of my outstretched arms.* He smiled as he stood with his back to the boy and pretended to reach for the snake.

"Oh Great *Yum Kaax*, god of our holy maize, I have been bitten!" screamed Ah Kan Mai. "Quick! Put the snake in this basket! Only its venom will bring the cure!" He pointed to the now stirring snake.

"But Your Holiness, I am afraid to touch it … it might bite …"

"If I die, Ah Tok, my blood is on your hands," Ah Kan Mai threatened, bringing his narrow hooked nose close to the servant's frightened face.

The hapless boy quickly grabbed the huge snake behind its head and raised it high as the whipping tail fought for control and its fanged mouth bit at the air. Trying to stop his crying long enough to concentrate, the boy lowered the angry serpent into the basket held forward by the priest.

At once, Ah Kan Mai clamped the top of the basket down and trapped the young boy's hand in the basket. He watched the boy's face wince in pain and then freeze in a look of horrible realization. Immediately, the boy's breathing ceased, and blood began to spurt from his nose, ears, and bulging eyes. Ah Kan Mai pulled the basket away and watched in fascination as the young victim gasped for air. The boy's face turned blue, and he collapsed to the soil of the cornfield.

What a short and unfortunate life. Perhaps they'll find him when the vultures begin circling overhead, Ah Kan Mai thought impassively, *but at least not until the mist clears.*

Hurrying back to the palace alone and carrying the heavy snake proved to be more tiring for Ah Kan Mai than the journey out to the fields with the young servant. On his usual ventures to the countryside to look for herbs, four young priests customarily carried Ah Kan Mai atop a litter. So this early afternoon, no one noticed the thin man hunched forward holding a basket close to his chest and laboriously climbing the numerous steps leading up to the palace complex.

No one noticed except Chukah Nuk T'zi. Jerky, furtive movements always attracted the attention of the giant man. A lifetime of silence had brought him knowledge of human nature not gleaned through the normal day-to-day activities of the average person. As he looked at the view of the valley from the hallway window just outside of Chanil's doorway, Chukah saw the priest emerge from the mist, struggle up the curving steps clutching a basket, and hurry across the courtyard below.

Chukah's finely honed senses came to attention. Something was wrong—not just with the priest who had now disappeared from view, but also something in the atmosphere. He stood still, smelling the air and listening beyond the strange silence. Something was about to happen—but he didn't know what.

CHAPTER FOURTEEN

The priest carried the basket to the southern wall of the lower courtyard and waited impatiently until two servants—the only witnesses nearby—had walked away. He quickly found his signal—the torch indicating an obscure and very low entrance to the hidden passage Lady Zac Ku had described to him. Although the old queen had revealed the location of this secret tunnel, the priest was glad she hadn't asked for the details of his plan. The less anyone knew, the better.

Ah Kan Mai descended a long, narrow tunnel beneath the palace and found the stairs leading up to the monarch's quarters—an escape route for the kings and their families, should they ever encounter danger. He left his torch in the wall-mounted holder and climbed through the side of a false window opening and down a short, narrow corridor barely the width of a man's body. Slipping through one more false window unseen from the outside, he found himself behind a stone column in the hall near the nursery. *Even I would never have known this opening was here,* the priest thought and scanned the area.

When Ah Kan Mai saw the huge back of the gigantic man who guarded the nursery and queen's rooms, he quickly hid behind the column. He watched K'in Balam's nursemaid leave the baby's room and saunter over to where Chukah stood. As she began to talk and gesture grandly to the silent man, Ah Kan Mai saw his chance.

In an instant, the priest entered the nursery. He quickly placed the deadly contents of his basket inside the sleeping baby's crib. He watched the killer snake slither under the infant's blanket. It only took moments for the priest to disappear back into the secret tunnel.

Ominous clouds hid the moon on its slow journey over the sun. As its path was set when the universe was created, so was the event that would occur simultaneously deep in the earth below. Just as the moon had fully covered the sun, the Great Turtle that holds the earth on its back in the sky decided to move.

As the sky darkened, Chukah Nuk T'zi heard the rumble before the earth actually began to shake. He bolted to the baby's room, and as he reached for the infant, he saw a slowly undulating movement under the baby's blanket. Faster than the snake could strike, he crushed the serpent in his massive grip. He grasped little K'in Balam to his enormous chest and ran to the center patio just as the terrible trembling began.

At first, an abrupt and powerful shudder shook the palace, followed by a rolling sensation that caused furniture and pottery to fall and shatter. The Great Turtle shook for several minutes, and the sounds of breaking items could be heard amidst screaming and confusion.

Chukah spotted the king and young queen emerging from the palace and waved to them. Chanil ran to Chukah and reached for her wide-eyed baby.

"When the awful shaking began, I had run to K'in Balam's room, dodging falling pots and plaster. Not finding him there, the king and I ran out here to the center patio, where we knew we would find you, Chukah. The king and I are grateful you were there to rescue little K'in Balam. Oh … there's my sister! Sak, are you all right?" she called as she ran to her sibling.

Watching Chanil kissing her baby was all the thanks the huge slave needed.

"Chukah." The king leaned in close. "I saw the crushed viper in my son's crib. Luckily, the queen didn't. I assume you were the one who saved the baby's life. I don't know how the snake got there, but I will do an investigation immediately. It seems you have saved my son's life twice today. I owe you my thanks. But I have one more thing to ask of you. Get rid of that snake. I don't want one of the servant girls to have to deal with it and tell the queen."

Most of the palace servants and priests had now collected in the patio, each one describing what they were doing when the temblor hit.

Captain Keh Cahal entered the patio with several soldiers to check for injuries and assess damage.

"Great Ahau, it seems you and your family have escaped harm. My soldiers have reported your rooms have little damage. May I send a few men to help put everything back in place?"

"Thank you, Keh Cahal, but our servants and Chukah here can take care of things."

"Captain," Queen Chanil interjected as she walked back to join them. "Please have your men check to see that the children of the city are safe and help any families that have suffered injury."

"Yes, Your Majesty ..." Keh Cahal began, but was interrupted by a frightened priest who ran up to the captain. "Is someone hurt?" the soldier asked.

"Yes. Although the walls of the priests' quarters have held firm, Ah Kan Mai fell down his tower stairs during the quake and is one of the few people bruised and bloodied. Many of his clay pots of herbs and liquids were scattered and broken, along with his divining mirror."

"I'll send a soldier back to the priest's tower with you. Cleanup shouldn't take long." Keh Cahal put a hand on the giant's huge arm. "And Chukah, we are all grateful for your quick actions. I don't know how you got out of the palace before things started falling, but you have saved the future king.

"Now, men," he called out, taking charge of the chaos. "Let's get this place back to normal!"

"Leave me alone. The gods have protected me. Just clean up this mess!" Ah Kan Mai ordered. He silently cursed the stairs, the stars, and the failure of his plans. He merely snarled when other priests came to the tower and bowed in reverence to his supreme knowledge of the horrific event he had predicted for this day.

I will wait. I am to be the savior of Palenque! Someday soon, I will have my chance, Ah Kan Mai thought to himself as he disappeared into his rooms to survey the damage.

CHAPTER FIFTEEN

Suspecting the high priest had brought in the snake, Chukah Nuk T'zi was bewildered how someone had secret access to the nursery. He felt responsible and vowed from that day on, no danger would befall the baby or Queen Chanil. He would be more observant of the crafty priest to better protect the infant and its mother. The giant had memorized the nursemaids' comings and goings, but he especially anticipated the times the queen came to her baby son's room. Her cooing and melodious voice spoke of pure love and happiness when she was with her baby.

Chukah Nuk T'zi had never heard such love from a woman. His poor adoptive family had little time to lavish love upon him. He didn't know why he was large and different from those around him. He knew his head was so huge, it resembled the Olmec statues found in the jungle. It was not shaped to emulate the sacred ears of corn, but was ugly and round. His nose was broad and flat across his face, and his body was wide and bulky, as were his chest, arms, and legs. His enormous hands were thick and square—twice the size of any other man's.

Chukah grew up hearing the story of how he came to live with his adoptive parents. They no longer had their daughter and were glad to welcome him as their son. He had heard from gossiping villagers that his mother must have died giving birth to a child as large as he. Chukah believed them and kept to himself as he grew, hoping to become invisible. But his size only brought curious stares.

His family lived far outside the city proper and beyond the upper-class homes that had easy access to the palace and marketplace. Chukah's family's home was simple, and like most other peasant dwellings, had plain walls of clay and a roof of palm fronds tied down and attached by ropes to the wooden ceiling beams. His happiest moments were listening to his family laugh and talk of the day around the home's hearth. The three stones creating the hearth, where the family meals were cooked, were the center of every Maya home.

Chukah's adoptive parents had been caring and nurturing. "I am always amazed how rapidly our son grows on our simple meals of beans and corn tamales. Maybe it is the corn I grind for his morning drink of *posol* or the chili powder I add to it," his mother would often tell the other women.

"My son, you are expected to work longer and harder in the fields than other children," his adoptive father, Moch Chuen, would tell him. Chukah went to work with his father at the building of temples as a youth because of his enormous body and strength. "Your size has saved you from being sacrificed, as most orphans are. There is always a need for sacrificial slaves and captives. We workers live in fear that we—or our children—will become Ah Kan Mai's next victims," his father would tell him angrily.

Chukah remembered the story his parents told of his little sister's death at the hands of Ah Kan Mai before he had come to live with them. The high priest determined that a young virgin's blood would appease the gods during *Uayeb,* the last five unlucky days of that *tun.* All were forced to watch her small body collapse under Ah Kan Mai's knife and to watch her blood burn in his holy bowl as he prayed for an auspicious new year.

The royal families, who descended from the sun and the hero gods, were growing in number, as were the upper class that catered to them. At the bottom, sustaining all the elite classes, were the peasants. They performed the backbreaking work in the fields, fought the wars with their bare hands, built the temples, and then gave their lives in sacrifice on the fearsome *chac-mool* stone.

When Chukah Nuk T'zi felt melancholy, he would close his eyes while his mind traveled far back in time. Bewildering memories showed him what this beautiful part of the world had been like before the kings, the squabbling upper class, the murders of helpless people, and before civilization went awry. His memory took him back generations before his birth. Voices told him he was a true Maya—one of the ancient ones.

He saw the beginnings of the Maya race, when Palenque was called *Baakal,* or Bone, before it was called *Lakham Ha.* In those bygone times, the first leaders—the tall, light-skinned *T'o'ohil* people—taught the smaller, gentle peasants how to build their glorious temples and grow corn and other crops. They patiently taught them how to read the stars and to know the seasons. They taught them how to make pottery, to count and write, and how to heal the sick. No one knew where these *T'o'ohil* people came from, but it was said they came from the stars. The duty of the priests was to teach each new generation of kings and priests the ancient secrets taught by the *T'o'ohil.*

Chukah saw how the rulers of Palenque were forgetting the original teachings. With each new reign, the priests, kings, and upper classes were devouring the land and its working class, just as a voracious swarm of *sak'al*—the army ants of the jungle—devours a helpless injured animal even before it is dead.

Chukah Nuk T'zi didn't know from where his ancient memories came, but he knew they were real and as true as Queen Chanil's love for her infant son. He could feel his queen truly cared for the people of Palenque. After the great shaking, he heard her ask Keh Cahal to send soldiers to help the peasant families who needed food and repairs. Chukah, in turn, would protect her and the baby with every ounce of strength his giant body possessed. He knew he was chosen by the gods to protect his queen, yet Chukah knew that it might mean going against the orders of the high priest who brought him to the palace. He would let the ancestors' voices in his head be his guide.

The next evening, Chukah's father, Moch Chuen, sat with a group of peasants in his home far outside the city's walls.

"I have received word that my son has saved the royal prince. The king and the gods will look with favor on him now. I suspect the snake he killed did not accidentally end up in the baby's crib. We all fear our king, who was descended from the gods, but there is someone in the palace that does not hold the same respect for our great *Ahau*. My spies will find out who did this and who was responsible for the death in the fields of Mol Kayab's son, young Ah Tok. Someday our people will be respected by the elite and no longer be treated as less than the insects who feed on our corn. But for now, we await that time."

CHAPTER SIXTEEN

AD 874

Queen Chanil sat in the cool breeze of the courtyard to escape the smoky air that had burned her eyes all day. This was the second day of the limestone burning to produce the cement used to plaster the new, artfully adorned walls throughout the city. She watched with pleasure as the king repeatedly swept their son into the air so high, the boy squealed and laughed with delight. It was clear K'in Balam idolized his father. At four *tuns* of age, he was dressed in little ceremonial clothes and looked like a miniature version of the king. Chanil had dressed him in a beautifully embroidered collar of many colors over his finely woven white cotton tunic. The jaguar skin wrapped around his tiny hips and tied at the side added to the regal attire befitting the boy's station.

K'in Balam loved to be in his father's arms. The king with his son was a familiar sight whether Akal held court with *sahals* or attended meetings with Keh Cahal and the priests. If the child got bored with the adults, the grassy courtyard was a safe place to play, as there were always plenty of servants or noble families to give him attention.

When the king left to return to the palace, Chanil sat K'in Balam on her lap and arranged his shoulder-length hair into smooth sections. She pulled the center portion up and back and joined the side portions high at the top of his head, wrapping his thick, dark hair with a deer hide strap. She gathered all of his hair into a tight bunch at the back of his neck and then secured that portion with another leather tie. "Now your hair is portioned into a beautiful jaguar tail here as it flows down your back. This handsome hairstyle allows me to see these small jade plugs in your ears.

"Sit still, my Little Sprout. It is time I replace these *tups* with slightly larger earplugs of the flower emblem that only royalty can wear. We will keep doing this until one day, your ears can take huge jade *tups* like those of your father. Our ears are portals to the soul, just as our eyes, nose, and mouth are. Our breath, voice, scent, and hearing are the expressions of our vital essence—our *ik*—just as the wind is the vital essence of the earth."

"But Mama …"

"Just one more moment, K'in Balam. I have to secure this second ear flare." She quickly tied its small leather cord that ran through the hole in his ear before the impatient child jumped from her lap.

"But my eyes are burning, and I want to go out and practice throwing the spear Keh Cahal made me," protested K'in Balam. "He has promised to take me hunting for turkey and deer! See, Mama, he is coming now!"

The imposing Keh Cahal approached. He was wearing a simple white *xikul*—a tunic of finely woven cotton fiber—a leather belt, and high-backed sandals. Even dressed so simply, Chanil could see why he commanded attention wherever he went.

"Your Highness, I thought I might take the Little Sprout out for a hunting expedition," Keh Cahal said as he bowed.

"I know you enjoy the highest reputation as a hunter, sir, but I worry about K'in Balam. We are cutting down and burning our forests more frequently. I find it distressing that it takes nearly two thousand *manzanas* of burnt forest to create enough limestone powder to cover just *one* building. I know we need to do this to also make room for crop fields, but we are disturbing vipers and rattlesnakes. There always seem to be more snakebites reported after we have invaded the forest. You will watch him closely?"

"I would consider it my duty, My Queen. And if you would like, your servant, Chukah Nuk T'zi, may accompany us."

"I trust you with my son, Keh Cahal. Perhaps we'll feast on turkey and squash tonight. And K'in Balam, I hope you will bring me more *cutz* feathers to sew on my robe. But if you can't catch a big *cutz* today, maybe you'll catch a squash for Mama!" Chanil laughed as she hugged her little son goodbye. "I will pray that Yah'ak Ah will guide your spears true to their mark. Our god of hunters and archers will appreciate a quail in offering tonight while we feast on *cutz*." Chanil waved goodbye and watched them descend the path leading to the valley. Later she would speak to the cook about possibly preparing a fresh turkey stew in *molé* sauce for the evening meal, but it was almost time for a very important meeting.

Chanil's servant girl, Muluc, excitedly parted the heavily woven red and blue draperies at the queen's doorway. She tried not to gasp at the strange, small person who stood there. Peering with eyes that could bore into the girl's soul was the *chilan*—the seer who was to read the futures of the queen and her sister.

Muluc had heard of another "different" courtier, the king's special servant years ago—a strangely shaped small man with a huge hump on his back. That little man was always in the throne room when the king was there. The hunchback's important job was to hold the king's divining mirror for him, but since his death, no other similar person had been brought to the palace. The servant girl believed that these unusual people had special powers, but she had never been this close to one of the *mas* people.

Trying not to look too shocked by the diminutive woman's peculiar presence, Muluc averted her eyes to the polished stone floor and motioned for the ancient dwarf in the brightly woven shawl to follow her into the queen's chambers. The girl knew the little *mas* people could naturally tap into the supernatural, and the reputation of this special, tiny old woman was revered throughout the palace.

The tall and stately young queen who greeted the old fortune-teller was younger and even more beautiful than the *chilan* expected. She had only seen this new Second Wife on state occasions with the towering, elaborate headdress and the stiff costume of her rank. Queen Chanil was now wearing a simple white *po't* and wore her long black hair in an unadorned braid down her back.

"Thank you for answering my summons, Na' Nuxi Ku. Your powers of *k'inyah* are well known here in the palace. We look forward to what your insights will teach us." Queen Chanil gestured to a small table in her bedroom.

The old *mas* limped forward, holding her bag of supplies. The queen's sister already sat forward on her stool, anxiously waiting for the session to begin. Chanil poured a drink of chocolate and chili powder for the wrinkled and toothless woman.

Taking her time, Na' Nuxi Ku opened her deerskin *pooxah* and dumped out its contents of broken pottery shards, hematite, bones, bits of mirror—the portals to the underworld—and yet another smaller bag. Opening the smallest pouch, the *chilan* took a pinch of a powdery substance and sprinkled it into her drink. The three women huddled together on small stools while the tiny fortuneteller stared at the seemingly ordinary contents on the little table.

Between gulps of the delicious beverage, her tongue slowly licked at the bits of chocolate that had dried at the corners of her mouth. *The new queen has the reputation of being fair to her servants, but how will she react to what I see?* wondered the old woman.

Na Nuxi Ku prayed aloud. "Itzamná, bless this reading, and may I see with clarity the future of your daughters before me." *The sister, although two* tuns *older than the queen, seems nervous and gossipy—something I will have to be careful of as I reveal their futures,* she mused as she avoided their curious stares.

Her collection of bone and stone bracelets clamored noisily as she pushed the broken pottery pieces into different configurations. She studied each piece in her dry, brown hands and waited for the powdered poison of the toad to begin its sacred work on her. Suddenly, the old woman's body stiffened, and her eyes rolled upward. She knew her actions created an eerie and spellbinding tension in the room. At last she spoke.

"Your place in Palenque was predestined, and your influence is crucial. However, I see darkness over you, My Queen. There are those who wish you harm. Although I see a snake waiting to strike, there is a giant jaguar guarding your door, so you have the blessings of the gods. Take precautions to protect your health, and accept these amulets to throw into the fire." She handed the queen a few of the polished stones from the table. With eyes still closed, the *chilan* paused to slurp her drink and poke some more at the bits of broken clay strewn about, somehow seeing through her closed eyes.

"Little Sprout will have a brother soon," she continued. "His new baby *yitz'in* will charm the gods with his flute. Bring more music to the palace for the baby to hear as he grows. Music is a sacred gift of the gods to men and an important element of the new child's upbringing."

Chanil hid her smile as she saw her surprised sister's eyes dart to her slightly protruding belly. "And what of K'in Balam?" the young queen asked.

The soothsayer chose her words carefully. "He will welcome a new playmate. It is good that he will begin to know the feeling of responsibility over a little brother. It is an education perfect for a future king who will know responsibility over his people."

All at once, the *chilan* saw the pottery and shells crumble into dust and blow away. Contemplating its portent, she brushed the ominous vision from her mind as quickly as she brushed her dry, graying hair away from her face. She didn't like how so many of the large pottery shards fell over the few tiny ones; these omens did not augur good fortune.

"What about me?" blurted Sak Ayi'in anxiously, breaking the spell. The *chilan's* eyes opened.

"You will marry and have a child as well, My Lady." The tiny dwarf's piercing stare shut off the sister's further probing. Turning back to the queen, the ancient *chilan* continued with her predictions for Chanil as she studied the tabletop. "The future king will be a great warrior. I see a spirit rabbit that helps you focus this boy's energies into using the gifts of his heritage toward his people and the precious land.

"Turn his impatience toward generosity and his quick mind toward understanding the people of Palenque, for they are more valuable than the priceless stones that dangle from your ears and neck, My Queen," the old crone advised. "I see great changes in the future of Palenque. The Maya people are hungry for more than just food.

"Perhaps I will be able to give you further insight at my next visit, when I have searched the underworld for more answers."

Sak Ayi'in shifted on her stool, ready to ask a question.

"I am through. I see no more!" Na' Nuxi Ku declared. She scooped up her divining tools into her *pooxah* and rose. Bowing as low as her feeble bones could accommodate, she accepted the valuable polished jade stone Chanil offered her and murmured the formal departing words, "*Bin in kah.* By your leave." The old seer avoided Sak Ayi'in's disappointed frown as she straightened her colorful shift, turned, and left the room.

Because the *chilan* always withheld bad news from the royals, she was still alive and revered for her talents. She would never have told them that upon entering the queen's room, she had observed a spirit bat fly over Sak Ayi'in. Furthermore, after her drink, she had clearly seen how Sak Ayi'in was laid out in her funerary attire, painted red with the cinnabar wash that represented royal blood and resurrection, and her body wrapped carefully in the soft gauze-like cloths used to prepare the bodies of the elite. Precious objects, clothing, food, and pottery surrounded Sak Ayi'in's lifeless body.

The old woman had seen Queen Chanil weep as she placed the bead of jade in her lifeless sister's mouth to nourish her on her afterlife journey. In the dead woman's arms, the old seer saw the newborn infant whose only purpose was to come to this world in the womb of Sak Ayi'in and to accompany her mother back to the underworld called *Cincalco*—the Home of the Maize. After that, the baby would travel to *Tomoanchan* to nurse at the many nipples of the Suckling Tree—to gain the strength to reincarnate.

The tiny old woman left the palace wondering what she would tell the queen's sister the next time she was asked to look into the future. She hoped that it would not be too soon.

"The *chilan* will return and spend more time with you, Sak Ayi'in." Chanil hugged her sister. "I didn't tell anyone of my condition because I wanted to see if she was truly as knowledgeable as the priests proclaimed."

"Well, it won't be a secret any longer," laughed Sak Ayi'in. "I'm sure the servants had their ears open near the doorway to hear her every word! Does the king know?"

"I think he suspects. I notice he has had all of my favorite dishes prepared for each meal." Chanil smiled, remembering how he had looked at her with such tenderness after their last lovemaking. He had pressed his large and calloused hand ever so gently over her belly and thanked her for bringing new life to his old bones. She suspected his priests had predicted he would have another son that *tun*.

Ah Kan Mai sat in his dank room beneath the observation tower where he kept his personal cache of herbs and enema pots. He had known of the coming birth before anyone. These many months, he had been lying low and focusing on keeping the trust of the king above all things. He was anxious to gain the confidence of little K'in Balam as well. Soon enough, it would be time for Little Sprout's lessons to begin.

Children are as clay and can be molded, just as an incense pot is formed to hold the precious pom *from the copal tree. And as the incense burns and sends its pungent smoke skyward, obliterating all other smells, what I put in the little prince's brain will burn as his truth, expunging all other teachings! The future king will burn with my passion, think as I do, and do as I say. Soon I shall rule Palenque, and he will be my little puppet.*

Keh Cahal watched his young charge as the boy hurried to keep up with him. The soldier relished his moments with K'in Balam. At times like this, he wondered what his life would be like with a son as bright and handsome as the future king, who was now struggling to keep his arrow steady in the miniature bow Keh Cahal had carved for him.

"You have shown me a real talent with your spear, and now I am seeing strong hands with the bow. Let us now use your new bow and arrow on a target. We must keep very quiet and wait for the pair of *cutzs* that come here regularly to eat. I have seen them in this clearing for the past two days, so I have sprinkled corn all around for them to enjoy as their last meal," he explained. "They are always in pairs—the male with his mate. They come to the same feeding place every day, even if they were frightened away from here before. Although they don't have the intelligence of the monkey or the speed of the fast and sleek *balam* you are named after, they fly very fast and close to the ground. So you must be ready. *Shhh!* I hear them now."

A fat male turkey with the red, brown, and blue plumage favored in ceremonial capes and headdresses appeared in the clearing. The colorful feathers glistened in the sunlight while the oblivious bird feasted on corn. As the male's less dazzling mate appeared, Keh Cahal gave K'in Balam the signal to shoot the female while he took aim at the male. His arrow shot with lightning speed through the air, finding its mark at the base of the male's neck and startling the female. K'in Balam's arrow pierced the female's thigh, but she took flight. Keh Cahal quickly used his bow to end her pain at the expense of diminishing the boy's hunting attempt. In an instant, she was down. They ran to their prizes and knelt to inspect the birds.

"K'in Balam, you did well with your new bow and arrows! For this prey, arrows are faster than a spear. You have good aim, even in an emergency. I am proud of you. Do you know why I had to shoot the female?"

"Yes, Keh Cahal. My mother tells me no one should suffer at the hands of a king, so I guess she also means a *cutz*. Anyway, I don't think I would like eating a turkey that I caused to suffer pain."

Keh Cahal loved the boy even more. "So! Your mother has the turkey she was hoping for. You will feast tonight! We now give thanks to Yah'ak Ah for our bounty."

CHAPTER SEVENTEEN

Although Men Lamat wanted to be there for Chanil and her son, now more than ever, he knew his life would come to an end in a few *tuns*. His journeys to the spirit world brought him visions of an aged rabbit being swallowed by a snake, and he knew he was the helpless rabbit. Sadly, the old man stood in the doorway of K'in Balam's classroom and watched Itz'At teaching the little boy how to use a paintbrush on bark paper.

Years ago, when plans were being made for Chanil's life in Palenque, despite the fervent protests of his family, Men Lamat had relished the thought that no matter how arduous the journey, he would see his brother's daughter become queen of the most beautiful of the Maya city-states.

As brother to King Hasau Chan K'awiil II, Men Lamat was an important priest of Tikal. Their other brother, Chanil's father, Ah Mac, chose to enter the military and became a fearless general. Men Lamat coveted neither the life of his brother, the king, nor the glory of war. His quiet studies brought him peace, and watching his royal charge grow into adulthood under his tutelage brought him joy. He attended to Chanil's education as she grew from a quiet, long-legged little girl to the lovely and regal young woman who had bravely faced a new life in a foreign city. She was always quick at her lessons and begged to know more about numbers, the calendar, and the art of writing. Her uncle, the king, proudly showed her first attempts at calligraphy to any visiting nobles. Whenever he could, King K'awiil encouraged her to tell him about the gods who resided in the heavens, thus allowing her to practice her knowledge on him.

When Chanil was just six *tuns* old, her father was killed in battle. Later that same sorrowful *tun*, her distraught mother, Lady Ton Kul, took a drink made from the poison of the *chechem* tree of the rain forest and ended her life. The old priest suggested that an aunt take charge of Sak Ayi'in's lessons while he personally concentrated on instructing his favorite niece, Chanil. It was evident from her birth that she was a true descendant of the royal Mayas of the past. Her fair skin and tall, long-limbed body was the replica of those truly descended from the gods. He wished for her a future that was worthy of her royal Maya heritage.

When Chanil was but sixteen *tuns,* Men Lamat's hope was to convince Tikal's king to have his beautiful niece seated near him at the approaching Council of Kings banquet. The old man knew the combination of delicious food, jugs full of fermented *balché,* and the exquisite, virginal Chanil Nab Chel would make King Akal Balam of Palenque dispel talk of war and be most eager to forge a stronger alliance with Tikal. He waited until he and the king were alone finishing their evening meal.

"Hasau, my brother! You are to have the three other high kings of the Mayan Empire here soon to meet and discuss the problems and policies of the twelve city-states over which all of you rule. Might I suggest that our beautiful niece, Chanil, accompany you and Lady Twelve Macaw at your first banquet? I think King Akal of Palenque would find her an intelligent and perfect banquet companion."

"What is going on in that intellectual head of yours, Men Lamat?"

"We are weary of wars, Hasau. I can see that Tikal's confidence is waning, and new construction has all but ceased. The opportunity to emerge from a downward spiral can present itself in the form of a fair and innocent young girl. You can provide the answer for Tikal as well as set Chanil's future as a queen rather than as a mere nobleman's wife."

"Are you suggesting, Men Lamat, that I try to convince Akal to marry our niece? I don't think I want her so far away in Palenque. I enjoy her company here."

"But soon, you will be approached by one of our noblemen for her hand in marriage," the older man reasoned. "Is anyone here in Tikal worthy of her? I believe I have successfully raised a queen and would gladly go to Palenque to continue her education and that of her children. So you see, Hasau, she won't be so very alone, and I'm sure her sister, Lady Sak Ayi'in, also would be happy for a chance to accompany her."

"Now you want both of my favorite nieces with you in a foreign city!" the king laughed. "Well then! Let us make sure Lady Chanil is in attendance at the Council of Kings banquet," said the king. "It appears King Akal's future is set already!"

Men Lamat's plan worked. Barely two days of the Council of Kings had passed, wedding plans were being discussed, and the gifts of Tikal's treasure houses were being arranged. Proudly, Men Lamat watched his obedient niece hide her fear of the unknown and bow to the king as he revealed her fate.

With love in his eyes that day, the king proclaimed, "Lady Chanil Nab Chel, you are to become a queen of the great city of Palenque. You shall represent the city of Tikal and her people. When you enter Palenque, they will be so taken by your beauty, it will be as though you were my one-woman army! But if harm comes to you there, our army shall devour them as surely as if we had marched on the city and taken them in the war they want so desperately to prevent. My brother, Men Lamat, shall accompany you to Palenque and teach your children as he has taught you. Lady Chanil Nab Chel, may the gods protect you on your journey and throughout your life as the Queen of Palenque."

Men Lamat stood, watching Chanil's son learn what a royal prince of Palenque must know. Despite his old age, there was still time for him to prepare Chanil's firstborn, K'in Balam, for royal duties. Although the child was only five *tuns* old, he was precocious and ready to learn, just as his mother had been at that age. Always inquisitive, he asked countless questions about each lesson, and that day's was no different. The old man watched K'in Balam as he sat on Itz'At's lap, ready to study the beautifully painted words describing the history of the Maya. The folded bark paper codex, which was coated with lime plaster and enclosed in a jaguar skin jacket, lay on a table in front of him.

Opening the codex, Itz'At began to explain, "Itzamná, the progenitor god, was also the first priest of the great Maya people. He invented writing and books. Our printed language is sacred and links us to him as well as to the other two gods of the sacred Triad.

"We have about eight hundred symbols, so you and I will be studying our sanctified writing for quite some time," the young scribe explained carefully, checking to see how much his little student was absorbing. "You will learn the holy symbols for words and for sounds ..."

"But Itz'At, how will I ever learn the meanings of all of these pictures?" interrupted K'in Balam.

"You are a smart boy and will learn, I promise you. It really isn't too difficult to learn our written language. We have two ways to express words. A drawn symbol can mean a word. For example, this glyph of a very obvious jaguar head stands for your name, *Balam*. However, a combination of symbols form individual sounds, creating a written word. These symbols for *balam* here with the dots representing jaguar spots and this symbol for the word *na* combine to mean your name. How it is written depends upon the artist doing the writing and the holy meaning behind each word." The boy studied the jaguar head glyph and smiled, clearly proud that such a beautiful character meant his name.

"As you know, our books are made of pleated bark paper. One very large page is folded into long pleats, becoming smaller, narrow pages. Our writing is to be read by beginning at the top left of the left-hand page. We read the symbols downward, two columns at a time, move up to the top of the page again, and read to the bottom once more. Then we move on to the page on the right. When we are through with that page, we fold it back to the left, and so on, until we reach the end of the first side of folded pages, like this," he demonstrated.

"There ... do you see the text on the back as well? We simply turn the book over and begin again, reading first on the left side, then the right, until we reach the end of the codex.

"When you are ready, I will show you how the fig bark is boiled in lime water—the same type of water in which we prepare our corn. I will also teach you how to draw our language with your own set of brushes. We will go to the marketplace so you may choose your very own red and black paint pots and seashell bowls."

"When you have finished this one," Men Lamat interjected, "I have many more codices for you to study. It is very important that you know the history of the Maya people, and particularly the history of Palenque.

"After you finish this book, we will take a break for lunch. I can almost smell those tamales being prepared for us, Little Sprout."

"Why is corn so important to the Maya people, Great Uncle? We eat it every day. Why didn't the gods make *chocolate* sacred instead of the corn?"

"Both are very important, K'in Balam. If you remember from your studies, at the beginning of our history, K'awiil sent a bolt of lightning to split a sacred mountain, and in so doing, revealed a maize plant and a cacao plant. That is why the maize god is also revered as our cacao god.

"Although the *cacao* bean doesn't need us, we work hard to get the seeds from the pod. We clean them, allow them to ferment, dry them out in the sun, and grind them on *metates* to form the powder we add to our drinks, our sauces, and mix with honey for your treats, my Little Sprout. We pray to Ek Chuah, our god of cacao trees, to provide us with this healthy and hearty food. But the gods, in their infinite wisdom," the old priest smiled, "came from the sky and gave us the corn.

"The corn needs us as much as we need the corn. If an ear of corn fell to the ground, it would not automatically work its way into the soil, as so many seeds do. The kernels are embedded in the cob and held there firmly by the outer leaves—the husk. So we carefully work to release the corn to be used to eat or to plant. Each kernel we *don't* eat must be dried and planted in carefully prepared soil to grow into a plant that produces *many* ears of kernels. But before we can eat the corn, we have to soak the corn kernels in a powdered lime and water solution to soften them.

"As we consume the sacred food each day, we remember how the great Maya people were made by the gods. They made us by mixing their blood with the white and yellow corn mush. Never forget: just as we are born, live, and die, so does the holy corn. We need the corn for our food, and the corn needs us to burn the old stalks and to plant the new kernels from the dried corn into the ash-rich soil. And so, as with the corn, you as king must need your people as much as they need you."

Men Lamat knew his advice to this future king was important in the short time he had left, because another teacher was waiting to corrupt this precious young mind. If only he could protect the future king from Ah Kan Mai.

CHAPTER EIGHTEEN

Chanil knew Ah Kan Mai looked for reasons to perform sacrifices at the steps of the Great Temple. She didn't want to be there. She disliked the high priest and didn't trust him. He seemed to relish the torture and killing of people. It didn't matter to Ah Kan Mai if his victim was an older adult, an innocent peasant, an enemy soldier, or a tiny child.

Attendance at the *Chac-Chac* ceremony was considered imperative by the monarchy to set an example for the people. Since early morning, the conch shell blasts alerted the city that all were to attend. Farmers, builders, servants, and nobility gathered before the Great Temple steps to watch the high priest perform his holy duty. The peasants stood behind the upper class, straining to watch in both horror and relief that it was not one of them this time.

In the heat of the late morning, the high priest was in the middle of a lengthy discourse on how the gods had been punishing the people of Palenque with snakes in the palace, frightening earthquakes, and lack of rain. Since the large quake many *tuns* past, smaller temblors shook the region with regularity and were a frightening reminder that the Great Turtle was still not sleeping.

"I have communicated with the Rain God, *Cha'ac,* our god of storms and sacrifice." He addressed the crowd. "Through these divine communications, it has been revealed to me it is time to satisfy *Cha'ac* with the fresh heart of a slave. Bring our gift forward!" he commanded of his attending priests.

As Ah Kan Mai stood at the bloodstained sacrificial *Chac Mool* altar, two priests presented a quivering, wide-eyed slave. The victim's upper body had been painted blue to ward off evil spirits, and his hands were tied behind his back. As censers burned, the beating of drums and chanting of the people almost drowned out the screams of the drugged, yet still frightened human offering as he was forced to kneel. The High Priest grabbed the unfortunate man's hair and pulled his head back, revealing a bare chest ready for Ah Kan Mai's finely chiseled knife.

Over the noise of priests drumming and chanting and the citizen's prayers, Ah Kan Mai's sonorous voice prevailed. "Oh revered God of the Rain, may our gift please you, nourish you, and satisfy your hunger. May you awaken from your sleep and look kindly on us from your paradise of Tlaocán. Send our land a cleansing rain!"

As the four elderly *chacs* held the terrified victim down on the raised stone *Chac Mool,* Ah Kan Mai took his obsidian blade and expertly made a swift incision in the center of he man's chest. The high priest reached in, and after carefully slicing each artery, extracted the warm heart, which he held up for the chanting crowd to see. It appeared as though the poor slave saw his own heart before he fell convulsing off the platform. The stillness of death did not come immediately.

Chanil watched the high priest's excitement as he held a pulsing heart in his hands. She shuddered with disgust, surmising that because of his blissful expression, under the heavy robe his hidden manhood stood erect with power. With a look of fearsome bliss, he placed the fresh heart in the *lac* containing incense and lit the contents of the bowl with a torch, sending the offering skyward.

Chanil struggled to keep her expression impassive. She hated these ceremonies, and her delicate stomach protested wildly. She could feel the sun's intense heat through her parasol. The smell in the air was sickening.

Not able to withstand the agony any longer, she clutched her stomach and ran into the temple, down the back steps, and hid behind a wall while she heaved her morning meal. Untying the chinstrap, she removed her heavy headdress before slumping on the grass in the cool shade of the temple.

Chanil didn't hear Keh Cahal's approach. "Are you ill, My Queen?" he asked softly. "May I call for your servants?"

"No, please just let me rest here a moment," she answered, embarrassed at her vomiting and self-conscious that she probably appeared less than queenly. Chanil reasoned it shouldn't matter that her husband's closest confidant saw her in this condition. "The child I carry has other plans for me than to watch yet another murder by the high priest." Knowing she sounded treasonous, she didn't apologize, but asked, "Why are you here, Captain?"

"I don't enjoy watching our high priest take his time sacrificing a slave either, Your Majesty. I am on my way to prepare plans for the next war council with Akal. If you do not need my help, then I ask your permission to leave you at rest here in the shade of the temple, My Queen."

The soldier bowed deeply and walked in the direction of the palace. "Tell my husband his unborn son protests the killing of innocent people!" she called out to him with conviction. Not knowing why she felt empty with his departure, she sat sobbing until she was ready to once again wear the composure of a queen who wanted for nothing.

Chukah Nuk T'zi waited until Keh Cahal reached the far end of the courtyard before he approached his queen sitting on the grass. He had seen Keh Cahal run toward her and heard their conversation. He didn't know why he heard her thoughts just as loudly in his mind as his own. As he watched her at the grisly ceremony, his own head swam with confusion. His stomach churned with nausea as he watched her bolt through the temple. Now she sat sobbing, and his heart ached at the sight of his regal queen crumpled on the ground and crying like a helpless child.

Suddenly, Chanil sat upright. "Chukah, is that you?" She turned to look toward the shadows of the temple. He bowed, walked to her side, and gently lifted her to her feet.

"I don't know what came over me. Is the ceremony over yet?" He shook his head *no* as he placed her headdress back on her head. Tying the chinstrap securely, she added in a lowered voice, "I will never understand how a human heart will convince the gods to send rain. As soon as little K'in Balam can understand, I am going to make sure he values human life. I am ready to return to my rooms, Chukah. Thank you for your assistance."

The giant accompanied his queen back her rooms. He was glad to escort her away from the sacrifice of a poor, defenseless slave at the hands of the high priest. Chukah looked at his own hands. How easily they could end the life of Ah Kan Mai, as they had the snake in K'in Balam's crib. But he knew that was not his task. Not yet.

Keh Cahal was back in his small quarters near the *Zac Nuk Na* building. Known as the "white skin house," it was the only white structure in the palace proper, as well as its most sacred. The outside walls were painted white with patterns of stylized red flowers and emblems of orange and blue painted in rows, allowing a striking contrast to the palace's other buildings of red and blue. The king and his council met to plan their war strategies there, or if the weather was stifling, in the adjoining courtyard.

Although Keh Cahal lived in the elite residential compound near the palace, he spent a great deal of time in this room, where he could feel grounded by his collection of war treasures and his weapons and uniforms alongside those of the king.

He felt unsteady, as if the Great Turtle were moving again. Keh Cahal remembered how Queen Chanil Nab Chel was the first person he had thought of when the big earthquake hit, and he recalled the great relief he had felt when he saw her emerge unharmed from the palace to run to the giant slave who held her baby. Since then he often thought about her rare smile. Now she glowed with exceptional beauty, no doubt from the child she carried.

The soldier had to admit to himself he had been watching her more and more lately. He had watched her at today's murder, as she called it. She stood regally beside the other royal household members as Ah Kan Mai performed the rain god ceremony. Her simple *po't* was accented with the brilliant hues of reds, blues, yellows, and greens in the shawl she wore over her netted collar of woven jade beads. Her headdress of long *k'uk* feathers and precious jewels drew all eyes toward her instead of Ah Kan Mai, who stood above the crowd, expecting to command everyone's attention. When Keh Cahal saw her eyes look downward as her hand reached to the wall for support, he knew something was wrong. When she ran into the temple, his army could not have stopped his running to her side.

Keh Cahal had never lacked the attentions of women who seemed naturally drawn to men of power. He enjoyed their company whenever he wished and knew he could marry the prettiest and wealthiest of maidens of the elite families. He didn't know what held him back. Perhaps it was the fact he was often away at war, keeping Palenque safe from invasion. Possibly he felt his first allegiance was to Akal Balam, and he was duty-bound to put the king's needs before a wife and family.

Or perhaps it was because all other women paled in comparison to Queen Chanil. He brushed that thought away and called out for his slave, Och Can. Not finding her and remembering she was probably still at the main plaza for the *Chac-Chac* ritual, Keh Cahal poured himself a cup of *balché*, the strong fermented honey and tree bark drink used for ceremonies. Holding it up, he called out, "To the King!"

But as he drank deeply, an inner voice saluted, *To my Queen!*

CHAPTER NINETEEN

C hanil stood at the throne room window looking out at the courtyard. She loved the sound of raindrops pelting the heavy awnings that kept moisture from entering the palace. Torrential rain and thunder had been shaking the palace walls since morning, and her skin felt sticky under her heavy costume. Perhaps Ah Kan Mai's ceremony did indeed bring the region the rain it needed.

She had dressed in a fine yellow gown accessorized with an ornate and heavy collar, beaded jade wrist cuffs, and belt. This was her "battle armor" for the confrontation with her least favorite palace resident. Over the years, the high priest had treated her with courtesy in front of others, but dismissed her as insignificant otherwise. Even over the thunder, Chanil heard the soft clinking of shells and knew Ah Kan Mai had finally decided to answer her summons.

"You requested my presence, Your Majesty." Ah Kan Mai spoke softly as he bowed to Queen Chanil. She had asked him to come to her rooms that morning, but now the high priest made it clear *he* chose this place and time. She had expected he wouldn't come, but if he did, Chanil was ready—and knew he would find her.

Chanil sat on the jaguar skin pillows of her throne just below the king's. Although Akal wasn't present, she had made sure her fan bearers and fly sweeps were there as witnesses.

The gaunt man stood before her, hunched like a vulture waiting for its quivering meal to finally succumb. His proximity made her skin feel as though tiny insects were crawling up and down her back. No wonder he was feared by most of the palace servants. She knew she must not let him see her apprehension and was glad Uncle Men Lamat had taught her how to appear detached and distant.

"I thank you for taking the time to visit with me, Ah Kan Mai." Chanil tilted her head in his direction in acknowledgement of his rank as high priest. "Although I have been in the palace for … has it been six *tuns?* We don't seem to have the opportunity to communicate often, and I wanted to make sure we are in agreement about how you will prepare K'in Balam for his accession rites. Would you care for a drink or something to eat?"

"No, Your Majesty. As you are aware, everything I consume—food or beverage—must be carefully chosen, as I keep my body pure for communicating with the gods."

"I understand, Ah Kan Mai, and I envy your willpower. It seems my body is hungry all the time. The child I carry dictates what I eat and when, and that seems to be everything and often!" She laughed and began to enjoy herself, knowing how it must peeve the high priest.

"Muluc, please bring me some of those wonderful tortillas I can smell cooking, and a cup of *ik'al cacao* … and both with plenty of chilies!" She allowed herself to savor the anticipation of her favorite chocolate drink with ground-up pink and white cacao blossoms before returning her attention to the wiry man still standing in front of her. She gestured for him to be seated one step lower than her bench.

"Now, back to K'in Balam's education. He has been studying his writing skills with Itz'At and my priest, Men Lamat. Both inform me the future king has a quick mind and is hungry for knowledge. Since you are careful about what you consume, I am sure you will understand King Akal and I are very careful about what knowledge now will influence our son's judgment as Palenque's future king. Tell me what you plan to teach him." Chanil smiled while imagining a thick stone wall between her and the high priest, just as Uncle Men Lamat had taught her.

She hoped she had caught Ah Kan Mai off guard; this was probably not a situation the priest had often experienced. Chanil could see beads of perspiration forming on his face. It must have angered him to fight for control in front of a young woman who was but one-third his age.

"Your Majesty," he began in a superior tone, "the esoteric education of kings is a vast knowledge that takes many *tuns* to comprehend. Although I had not thought about beginning K'in Balam's education until he had reached seven *tuns,* I am glad you understand its importance. Being an *outsider,* I presume you are unaware of our palace customs. The *king* will be informed when the time is right to begin. For the moment, the tutor, Men Lamat, will teach him skills appropriate for women and children. When I have divined the time of the boy's studies, Men Lamat's services will no longer be required." The queen's impassive face quickly changed to a radiant grin as the servant girl returned.

He paused while Muluc set down the tray containing a plate of warm food and the screw-top clay pot that contained the cacao drink. Muluc held the pot high and expertly poured the hot drink into a cup on the stone floor to produce the foamy drink enjoyed by her queen. Chanil felt certain the savory aroma of the food was making Ah Kan Mai uncomfortably hungry.

Perhaps it had. Not waiting to be formally dismissed by the young queen, he stood and managed a slight bow. "It seems our conversation is over for the time being. I will leave you to your nourishment, My Lady, as I am late for a meeting with my under-priests. Good day." The high priest turned his back on Chanil and left.

Chanil looked at her servant's stupefied expression and smiled. "I didn't want him for a meal companion anyway, Muluc. Please enjoy this beautiful food or find someone who is as hungry as I *was.*"

The young queen was aware of Ah Kan Mai's rudeness, but glad for his departure. She was also well aware of his insinuations. If Muluc's entrance hadn't interrupted them, Chanil wasn't sure if she could have retained her composure at Ah Kan Mai's imperious pronouncements. He was almost successful at making her feel insignificant.

Chanil had made her point this time, but dreaded the next encounter. She remembered the *chilan's* warning. Was Ah Kan Mai the "snake" that lay in wait for her? She had no proof of her suspicions, but for the present time, the young queen knew she was safe in the palace with protection from the king, Chukah, Keh Cahal, and the company of her sister and servants. In the meantime, her most important duties were to her husband, son, and unborn baby.

Chanil walked back to her rooms along the large outside colonnade that allowed a panoramic view of the lush valley below. The rain had stopped. She paused to look down and watch the farmers working and then turned to touch the *Yax Tun,* the huge, unpolished jade boulder that sat along the walkway. It was taller than her height and must have taken twenty men to bring it there. The stone always felt warm and alive to her. Its carefully executed carvings chronicled the dates of the most impressive wars and feats of the past kings of Palenque. As she stroked the blue-green boulder, she thought of her husband and the tremendous problems he had to deal with. She knew her trepidations concerning Ah Kan Mai were too small to add to the king's stresses now. She decided to head for the comfort of Uncle Men Lamat's rooms.

Men Lamat bent close to his stack of codices. When the old priest saw Chanil enter his room, his decrepit body straightened slightly, and he grinned in delight.

"You are even more beautiful in this pregnancy, Chanil," her old teacher said as he bowed low and responded to her embrace. "May I tempt you with some midday nourishment?" he asked as he smiled even more broadly, already knowing the answer.

"Of course, Uncle. I have just had a small battle, and now I am very hungry. I crave chaya leaves and scrambled turkey eggs sprinkled with toasted pumpkin seeds! Let's have them bring you quail meat and egg yolk tamales. Please join me, Uncle, for you are looking much too thin lately," she added as she took his hand. "You know the king's second son will need your strength and expert guidance as well." Chanil suddenly looked serious.

"Well, we will not begin the new child's lessons on the positions of the stars until he is at least six moons old, Chanil." Men Lamat joked as he tried to make her smile again. He gave his servant their food orders and waited until he was sure they were alone.

"Tell me, My Queen, where have you done battle today?" the old man asked quietly.

"Last night, Akal and I were speaking about K'in Balam's education. I have not confronted Ah Kan Mai directly since my arrival here, so this morning, I decided to speak to the high priest about our son's further training toward kingship. He didn't grace me with his presence until just a little while ago. It apparently was not a subject he felt concerned me, and he explained that the *king* would be advised when the time was right for K'in Balam's training to begin. Uncle, I felt as though I was fighting for all I was worth to retain my composure at his declarations of power. The air in the room felt heavy with his presence."

"You are very observant, Chanil. He was using his magic powers to try to subdue you. But you are a true Maya, and I am sure he found you a formidable presence. You may have angered him further, but your fate is in the hands of the gods, so continue to pray and offer your sacrifices.

"As far as K'in Balam is concerned, you are teaching your son to be a strong and independent thinker. Your job as a mother is to raise children who are capable of clear thinking on their own. It is possible both boys may rule together as adults, which is not unusual here in Palenque. It isn't a bad idea to teach boys about food, herbs, and medicine, such as women know. As you may remember, I taught you many things that are taught to boys. If you apply this advice, your children will not be as dependent on other people for survival. We don't always know in whom we can trust."

Their warm food arrived, and they ate and chatted comfortably. But Men Lamat had much on his mind.

"It is time you rested, Chanil. That son you carry will be here soon, and you need your strength." Men Lamat squeezed her hand and sadly watched her depart. Perhaps the time had come for the old priest to also confront Ah Kan Mai. Men Lamat had been schooled in the magic arts and was curious just how powerful the high priest's knowledge was.

It would soon be time to know the enemy.

CHAPTER TWENTY

Things were beginning to cycle beyond the control of Ah Kan Mai. The young queen was now pregnant with the king's second son. The old queen had all but given up on fighting for matrilineal control, and her useless daughter, Yax Koh, was still failing to conceive. The giant employed to control the queen was a mere statue at her door. Perhaps he was witless as well as speechless. Ah Kan Mai had to take matters into his own hands.

There were unsettling rumors from the vassal city of Toniná in the southern territories. A visit there from the royal couple would be a good excuse to get the queen away from the palace and the protection she enjoyed from all sides. Lady Chanil was much too sheltered at home. The high priest needed a location away from Palenque to be able to create the ideal setting for a tragedy. After a frightening dream of his drowning, he formulated a plan for the perfect place to finally rid Palenque of the queen.

Ah Kan Mai had waited patiently for the ideal opportunity to approach the king about a trip far from the palace. Only the king, his fan bearers, and the king's scribe were in the throne room that day.

"You appear deep in thought, Ah Kan Mai," the king said as the high priest approached the throne with a bow.

"Your Majesty, I have been hearing troubling whispers about Toniná of late. One of my under-priests has relatives there, and he has informed me of the gossip spoken in the palace. May I suggest a visit to Toniná in the near future to dispel the rumors saying you have lost control of them? They allow gossipers to spread stories about how their governor is weak and their priests are powerless. Perhaps a trip there with the new queen will show her how you remind your subjects of the proper way to worship the two of you since your marriage."

"That is an interesting idea, Ah Kan Mai," pondered Akal.

"And why not travel farther south to Chinkultic as an extraordinary destination to show your queen the *cenote* created by the gods? Surely a special ceremony and sacrifice at that sacred pool will put you in favor with our water god, *Cha'ac*. I know you must wish for the god's blessings for your new son, who is to be born this *tun*."

King Akal appeared to give these plans some thought. "Ah Kan Mai, your suggestion is a good one. My beautiful Chanil has not left the palace since arriving here many *tuns* ago. I will speak with her and her uncle, Men Lamat, about a trip."

"Oh, Your Majesty, allow me to suggest that her old priest might not be up to such a journey. Perhaps it would be best if he stayed here to continue with K'in Balam's education and to be company for the queen's sister. May I also recommend that the giant Chukah Nuk T'zi might better serve Your Majesty here in the palace to guard the Little Sprout? A few soldiers, my priests—and of course myself—will be sufficient protection for you and the queen."

"I believe your ideas are sound, Ah Kan Mai. I know you have my family's best interests at heart. I will consult with Keh Cahal for the best time to travel with a few of his strongest soldiers, and I expect you to ascertain the most auspicious dates for this journey. I look forward to showing my new queen the beautiful city of Toniná, and the visit to Chinkultic will be a highlight, with its special blue water sacrificial pool in the middle of the jungle."

Ah Kan Mai felt ecstatic at the thought of planning how he would rid Palenque of its infection introduced by the king's marriage. The young queen would be a perfect offering to *Cha'ac* in Chinkultic's *cenote*. The journey would last at least one *uinal*. The traveling party would return to Palenque in one moon *without* their temporary new queen, and the high priest could resume his plans for control of his beloved city.

⋘❦⋙

"Dearest Akal, I look forward to this journey you have arranged. Although I can't imagine leaving K'in Balam for a whole moon period, I know he will relish being spoiled by Sak Ayi'in, Uncle Men Lamat, and the servants. It will be enjoyable spending this time with you and learning more about the lands you rule." Chanil checked her pile of clothing for travel and for ceremonies. She preferred to choose her own travel items and accessories and place them on her bed for Muluc to clean and repair. The young queen stood tall and arched her back to relieve the ache she felt at the base of her spine.

"Are you feeling all right, my love?" The king looked concerned.

"Yes, Akal, I think I'm just tired today. So you believe this is a good time to take this trip?"

"Yes Chanil, I do. This journey will be a goodwill visit to the troublesome Toniná. It is halfway between Palenque and Chinkultic. Keh Cahal tells me we will travel on foot southeast from Toniná to the Lacantún River. From there, our *kayuks* will take us to a point within two days of Chinkultic. I hope this trip won't be too tiring for you in your condition. But Ah Kan Mai has reminded me that the sacred *cenote* there is the perfect place for the two of us to have a special ceremony."

Chanil brushed aside the troubling warnings from Uncle Men Lamat and Sak Ayi'in earlier that day.

"Why can't I go with you? I would love to get out and see the Maya lands, too." Sak Ayi'in looked as though she wanted to cry.

"But I need you here with K'in Balam, Sak. Perhaps he won't miss me too much if you are company for him." Chanil tried to soothe her sister.

"I also feel uncomfortable about your leaving on a journey now that you are expecting again, my sweet Chanil," added Men Lamat. "One *uinal* is a long time to be away from your midwives and family."

"You both worry too much," she said, and she tried not to think about their warnings.

I'll miss them and K'in Balam, Chanil thought as she returned to her packing. *I have never been away from my son more than a few hours. I can't imagine how I will go one uinal without his hugs and kisses. But this time with Akal is very important. Lately he has been so preoccupied. I miss the days when he shared stories of his life. Perhaps this journey will give us time alone to recapture the past.*

Within five days, the traveling party was ready and poised for their journey. Captain Keh Cahal warned that leaving later might put them in danger of bad weather. Chanil had begun feeling pains similar to her monthly cramping and had also begun to feel more tired lately. Not wanting to worry her loved ones, she kept her discomfort and nagging foreboding to herself.

"Mama, why can't I go with you?" K'in Balam cried as Chanil hugged him one last time.

"You are going to be so busy, you'll hardly notice I am gone, my sweet boy." Chanil smiled as she fought back tears herself.

Sak Ayi'in swept him into her arms, and the sisters brushed cheeks before the young queen stepped onto the litter awaiting her. With promises of bringing home interesting presents from foreign lands for everyone, the traveling party said goodbye and headed southward. Chanil strained to see Sak Ayi'in and K'in Balam waving goodbye from the Grand Avenue. She closed her eyes to impress that image in her memory forever and then turned to face whatever lay ahead.

Chanil was happy to have her servant, Muluc, along. The girl was quiet, yet reliable. Captain Keh Cahal was also visible now and then as he barked orders to his soldiers and made sure the travelers kept on course. Breathtaking vistas and lush jungles enchanted Chanil on the journey to the hostile Toniná. Even more delightful were her moments with Akal. She felt as though she was once again the young queen he instructed about life in the palace. He shared stories of battles and tales of Toniná's kings.

At times, Chanil walked along with Muluc, but was happy to lay back and ride when her back started aching. She was glad to be taking a trip away from the palace. It was good to have a change of scene, even though the view included Ah Kan Mai at times.

Entering Toniná, Chanil saw how the city was positioned against the foothills. She gazed upward in awe at its seven impenetrable levels facing south. Looking closer at the wall between the fourth and fifth levels, she shuddered at the striking stucco artwork of a fearsome turtle-footed god holding the decapitated head of ancient Palenque's Kan Hoy Chitan II, the son of Palenque's greatest king, Pakal. Seeing the wall relief reminded all of them of a dark time in Palenque's ancient history. Chanil closed her eyes and prayed that Akal would never experience this kind of fate at the hands of this war-mongering city.

A band of Toniná's soldiers led them on a tour of the city as they wound their way to the palace. Other depictions of executed enemies were displayed on walls and stelae throughout the public areas in realistic horror. The travelers were taken past the palace steps, one of which showed a carving of Palenque's K'awiil Mo' as captive. But they were also treated to friendlier views of the beautiful city, which included the two impressive ball courts, and of course, the striking blue and red painted palace. Elaborate banquets were scheduled, along with introductions to the city's nobility.

Ah Kan Mai was enjoying his status as Palenque's high priest. He was introduced to Toniná's high priest's son, a young man who clearly loved the drugs to which he had access much more than the discipline of a priest's life. It didn't take long to arrange a private meeting with the young man.

"Ben Maxam, I am looking for an apprentice whom I might rely on in Toniná to make sure this city and its governor obey the policies of King Akal Balam. Perhaps you are that person."

"Ah Kan Mai, I bow to your authority. Here, it is spoken of in whispers—that it is your leadership that rules Palenque and that the king would not make a decision without consulting you on your opinion."

The high priest smiled. "I cannot completely disagree with your assessment. It is true the king needs help with the vast lands he governs. He relies on my knowledge and communications with the gods. And in turn, I sometimes need help with my responsibilities. You appear to be a young man who could be of service to me—and therefore King Akal Balam. Perhaps you would also like to learn more about Palenque's pathways to the gods? Our sources are exquisite in their delicacy, yet powerful in the visions they reveal."

The high priest paused to assess the young man's reactions. It was obvious his new friend couldn't wait to find out more about Ah Kan Mai's cache of drugs. "In fact, I have brought several opiates with me to use in my ceremonies during this journey. Tonight, let us meet away from the others after the banquet. I will share with you some of my best gifts from Palenque, and we will also discuss how you may help me."

After the governor's dinner, which was much too rich for Ah Kan Mai's taste, they met in his elaborate guest room. The high priest waited until the servants were gone to begin his conversation with the young man. "Your city certainly entertains her visitors with generosity and beauty. I can tell how impressed King Akal was with tonight's banquet. I was not surprised his difficult young wife was not in attendance, as she has been in poor health lately, and honestly doesn't care to be friendly with people who are strangers to her. In fact, if I may say so—with your promise of complete confidence—she is not as beloved as the First Wife is."

"Is that so, Ah Kan Mai? I thought the people loved their new queen! How does the king handle the problem?" asked Ben Maxam.

"Honestly, the king cannot quell the rumors and gossiping about her. I sometimes feel he is embarrassed that he married a woman from Tikal. *Balché?*" he offered as he poured two cups of the beverage.

"Last night, I dreamed that swarms of beetles were attacking a huge field of holy corn. The sound they made was the same as that of a woman's cackle, laughing and laughing as they ate everything in sight. I looked on powerlessly and prayed to the gods. Just then, a flock of young and strong birds swooped down to feed on the insects, whose cackles became screams as the birds consumed every last damaging beetle! So, do you see the reason why I wanted to talk to you this evening, Ben Maxam?"

The slightly intoxicated young man looked perplexed.

"You are an intelligent and capable young man with many talents," Ah Kan Mai began carefully. "I know you want what is best for your own city and our great *ahau,* King Akal. I am about to bring up a delicate subject, but I trust you." The high priest looked around to make sure they were completely alone. "I ... *we* need your assistance in ridding Palenque of its interfering queen."

"But Ah Kan Mai ... isn't that a drastic action? I don't see how I could ..."

"Ben Maxam, I am in constant communication with the gods, so it may be unfair of me to ask you, a novice priest, to understand how the great god *Cha'ac* would appreciate the most supreme gift that could be offered—Palenque's pregnant queen in exchange for an eternity of glory and good fortune for Palenque and for Toniná." Ah Kan Mai revealed his most pious expression.

"But most esteemed Ah Kan Mai ... I ... it is a crime to harm a descendant of the gods! Surely you don't mean me to kill Lord Akal Balam's new queen ... I would be put to death for such an act!"

"Calm yourself, Ben Maxam," Ah Kan Mai whispered. "Palenque's real queen, Lady Zac Ku, is still the First Wife and the *true* queen of Palenque. We can't be sure this new Second Wife is even carrying the king's son. I have heard it whispered that she has been with others. Perhaps she carries the child of a soldier of Tikal." Ben Maxam gasped in horror.

Ah Kan Mai continued, enjoying his audience. "In my meditations, I have seen the child from her womb grow to become a strong soldier himself and one day leading an army that will destroy Toniná!" The young man's shocked expression was all Ah Kan Mai needed in agreement. "Now, if you will help me, our great *ahau* Lord Akal Balam, and Palenque, I will keep your shelves stocked with the finest powders and tinctures in my stores. Perhaps you would you like to try some now while we continue to discuss our options?"

CHAPTER TWENTY-ONE

After seven days in Toniná, the royal party from Palenque began passage by *kayuk* on the Lacantún River southward. At times, the rapids made travel quite rough, and Ah Kan Mai could see that the journey was taking its toll on Lady Chanil. In two short days, they arrived at the landing, where soldiers awaited their arrival and a cushioned litter awaited her for the final travel to Chinkultic. Although no one said anything, the high priest saw the blood stains on the lower back of her cloak as she left the *kayuk* to board the litter.

In the new city, Ah Kan Mai was not surprised those two days of sightseeing and banquets in Chinkultic had forced Queen Chanil to bed, and that she lay resting in her room at the palace. He knew this plan could now be set in motion.

"Tell your queen I have important information for her," he announced to her servant, Muluc. The girl returned and motioned for him to follow.

"Your Majesty, I hope I am not disturbing you." The high priest bowed low, his eyes taking in the queen seated at a desk, her unmade bed, and her frowning servant. "Are you unwell? I must say, the food here is quite heavy in spices and texture. I have some herbs that might make you feel better ..."

"I'm just resting, Ah Kan Mai. What is the reason for your visit?" Chanil appeared too tired to generate a polite smile.

"I assume you are enjoying your visit to Chinkultic? The *cenote* here is rare in this part of the king's territories. It is said that prayers offered to *Cha'ac* in this particular pool are heard and answered—if they are truly prayed in earnest. I am sure you want to do everything in your power to assure the safety of the child in your womb. It would be a tragedy if the baby were to be born prematurely." The look of alarm on Queen Chanil's face was all he needed to know his plan could work.

"After much praying, I have received a message from *Cha'ac* that he will give your child strength if you and the king only go to the sacred pool and pray to him under the full moon, which occurs tonight. *Cha'ac* has instructed me to give you these rare stones. Our rain god will appreciate these precious amulets. Throw them into the pool as you pray." Ah Kan Mai bowed again, handed Chanil the bag of stones, and turned to leave, but stopped. "Don't worry about informing the king; I shall tell him he must meet you there after tonight's banquet. Get some rest, Lady Chanil."

He quickly departed and headed straight for the palace's kitchen. Ah Kan Mai personally prepared a special tea for Lady Chanil and instructed the kitchen staff that this was to be given to her servant when she came for the queen's tray of afternoon tea.

Chanil pondered this strange and oddly friendly visit from Palenque's high priest after she asked Muluc to bring her favorite soothing tea.

"Muluc, rest is the most important thing for me now. Thank you for this pot of chaya tea. It is making me sleepy. Please have some as well and go lie down, as I am about to do. Our schedule has kept you as busy as the king and I have been. I think it is best I sleep to ease these cramps that are beginning to worry me. If the king returns here from his meetings, please tell him that I must speak to him about going to the *cenote* tonight. Although I have mentioned it to him, I have not had the opportunity to plan our ceremony. I wish you could come with me, but Akal and I must be there alone together."

Chanil lay down and thought about the special prayers she and Akal would perform. Ah Kan Mai said it was important they carry out the ceremony under the full moon. Another night would not be as auspicious. If she wanted to save her child from being born too soon, she must go tonight. She was happily surprised that the high priest was showing some concern over her, even if was only to insure the safety of the king's unborn child. That nagging feeling began forming in her mind once more, but at the moment, sleep was all she could manage.

❧

Ah Kan Mai had made sure the king was busy in meetings with Chinkultic's sahals all morning. After that, Akal's hectic schedule included observing the city's army with Keh Cahal, and now Ah Kan Mai joined the king to watch a late afternoon ball game.

As the men sat enjoying the game, Akal turned to his high priest. "Your suggestion about this trip has proven successful, Ah Kan Mai. I have had important meetings with leaders, priests, and soldiers in both cities. Their fealty is once again secure. I am happy my queen has enjoyed herself, as well. I haven't seen her all day, and I look forward to a quiet dinner with her this evening."

"Forgive me, Your Majesty! Have I neglected to tell you of the extremely important banquet tonight with Chinkultic's governor and high priest? I ask your pardon for the mistake I made if I have overlooked informing you of this significant celebration in your honor. I am sure our hosts would understand the queen's absence tonight due to her present fatigue, but if you declined to attend ..."

Akal frowned. "Don't worry, Ah Kan Mai. I will be present at the dinner. But I would appreciate a break from all this entertaining. I'll go explain this evening's activities to the queen now."

"By all means, Your Majesty." The high priest bowed low.

Ah Kan Mai was confident the specially prepared chaya tea had done its work. The king would be unavailable to the queen at night, leaving her alone. The last part of his plan was the only variable. Would his new accomplice, the young priest from Toniná, make his planned appearance in Chinkultic?

❧

Akal approached the elaborate chambers prepared for them by the governor's staff. He entered to find his wife in a deep sleep and Muluc asleep on a pallet near her. *Hadn't she mentioned something about going to the sacred cenote tonight? Chanil has been tired for the past two days. It appears she won't be going anywhere. After she wakes, we'll plan the ceremony for tomorrow night. Now I suppose I must attend the governor's dinner.*

King Akal took one last look at his sleeping wife and reluctantly left the room.

Chanil awoke in the darkened chamber. It took her a moment to remember where she was. With a start, she recalled she was to go to the *cenote* to perform a ceremony! Where was Akal? Perhaps he was there already waiting for her. She arose unsteadily and grabbed the amulets Ah Kan Mai had instructed her to use. She stumbled out of the palace and into the darkness in the direction of the sacred pool.

Feeling an awful headache, Chanil struggled as she tried to clear her head on the way down the moonlit jungle path, accompanied only by the sound of owls singing to the heavens and the giant spiders whose positions in the trees were revealed on their glistening webs. She finally found the clearing where the beautiful circular pool shone in the light of the full moon.

It was breathtaking. Leaning in to peer into the blackness of the pool, she saw the incalculable stars reflecting their brilliance in the water. It was very peaceful there. Now Chanil knew why this pool was sacred. Only the gods knew how many countless gifts of sacrificed worshippers and priceless amulets lay forever within its dark, bottomless depths.

She stood there clutching to her breast the precious stones Ah Kan Mai had given her. "Oh, holy *Cha'ac,* please hear my prayer to you. I beseech you with all my heart and ask that your blessings be bestowed upon the child in my womb. My greatest fear is that this baby will be born too soon. Please protect him so that he grows to be a healthy son of your servant, King Akal Balam. I also ask for the king's protection and for our son K'in Balam's health and safety. Finally, I ask you to protect our beautiful Palenque and its people." She held out the amulets and had one last thought. "Oh, revered goddess Ix Chel, please protect your grateful daughter before you."

As the young queen leaned over the pool to throw the precious stones in, she saw her own reflection—and strangely, that of another person close behind her.

Has Akal come at last? Chanil smiled and turned to face him. But as she did, she was horrified to realize that an unfamiliar man was reaching for her waist. He was attempting to push her into the *cenote!*

With a scream, she turned and tried to fight his grasp. He put one hand over her mouth and forced her closer to the water. *I cannot let him push me into the* cenote! *He cannot hurt my baby!* Chanil struggled to force her body—and that of her attacker—away from the black pool. Although she was a head taller than he, his stronger muscles forced her backward. With all her might, she used her arms to push his upper body away. Her attacker was a young man she didn't recognize.

Then with a sigh, he released her. Chanil watched the young man grasp at the point of an arrow protruding from his chest. She stepped aside in horror as he looked up at her with a surprised expression and collapsed forward into the black pool.

"My Queen! Has he harmed you?" Keh Cahal sounded frantic as the soldier ran to her from the trees.

"Keh Cahal! No ... but he was trying to force me into the *cenote* ..." Chanil felt tears of fear and relief wash over her. Feeling as though she might faint, she reached for him.

"Why were you here alone, My Queen?" Keh Cahal held her gently.

"I came to perform a ceremony, thinking Akal would join me ... I hardly remember how I got here; I have been so tired ..."

"There must have been some misunderstanding. But I am here. I will always protect you," he whispered, holding her in his arms until she could stand on her own. "We must find the king and tell him what has happened."

❧

King Akal sat in the banquet hall in discussion with other men as the food was being cleared and yet more *balché* was being poured. The room went quiet. The king looked around and was surprised to see Keh Cahal and Queen Chanil approaching his chair.

"Your Majesty," Keh Cahal bowed on one knee and crossed his right arm over his chest. "The queen was just in great danger from a young man who was attempting to murder her!" Shocked comments began around the room but fell silent as the king exploded from his chair and ran to her.

"Are you hurt, Chanil?" he asked as he held her.

"No, Akal—thanks to Keh Cahal, who came from the forest to stop the man from … from …" She couldn't go on at the thought of what almost happened.

Keh Cahal continued for her. "I was on my way back to my room, Your Majesty, when I was approached by the queen's servant, Muluc, who told me she was unable to find Lady Chanil. The servant girl said the queen mentioned something about meeting you at the *cenote*. I knew you were here at the banquet, so I went there myself. As I came down the path to the sacred pool, I heard her scream and came upon an unfamiliar man attempting to force her into the water. My arrow struck him, and he fell into the *cenote*. This man wasn't one of ours …"

"Your Majesty," interrupted Ah Kan Mai, "it would be impossible to retrieve the man's body from the bottomless pool. Since we have no way to identify him, we cannot know for sure which responsible parties must be brought to justice. Perhaps Chinkultic's governor can explain why one of his citizens was trying to murder our queen!"

The shocked nobleman and his worried coterie of advisors huddled in a group and whispered about the consequences of a fanatic's actions. The frightened governor stepped forward and bowed low.

"Great Ahau … we know of no one who wishes you or your queen harm!"

King Akal walked with Chanil to the center of the room, and the crowd fell silent.

"Our visit to Chinkultic is over. I expect a full investigation of who this man was and who put him up to it by the time we reach Palenque.

My queen was almost murdered here in your city. Her health is delicate, and I will not allow harm to come to her or my son she carries.

"Keh Cahal, ready your men. We leave for Palenque tomorrow!" He took Chanil's arm and escorted her from the room.

Ah Kan Mai and Keh Cahal watched them leave. "The king's anger will not subside easily," muttered the soldier. "It seems our queen is now in danger. But she will be safe as long as *I* live!" His steps echoed on the stone floor as he hurried from the banquet room.

As Palenque's high priest headed for his own room, he pondered the surprising good fortune of the young queen. Perhaps the gods weren't yet ready to allow him to rid Palenque of her influence. The queen's attacker failed at his duty, but no one would ever know it was the young priest from Toniná. His bones would dissolve in the bottomless depths of the holy *cenote*. Perhaps Chac had decided it was the young man's sacrifice he required.

If young Ben Maxam's absence from Toniná is questioned, they will assume drugs had no doubt led him into the path of a hungry jaguar. The years have taught me patience. When the gods are ready to leave the young queen to me, no soldier or king can save her.

CHAPTER TWENTY-TWO

AD 875

Since the new royal birth, the palace was once again teeming with visitors to the queen's rooms. The baby prince's incredible wails sent servants scurrying for gourd rattles, carved wooden and painted clay toys, and honeyed sweets. Even Chanil had a hard time entertaining little Chan Kayum and keeping him occupied and quiet.

The queen rocked her crying baby and walked back and forth across the nursery floor. All who saw baby Chan Kayum noted that at only three *uinals,* he looked every inch a royal son. He wore his *sak hunal,* the princely white band around his little head, from which a jade bead hung to the bridge of his nose to encourage his eyes to cross. But his eyes were busy squeezing out enormous tears as he balled up his little fists and wailed at the top of his lungs.

Chanil breathed a tired sigh and sat next to her sister. "I'm exhausted! The *x'mans* have assured me he is not ill. Although his *sih* was not as difficult a birth for me as that of K'in Balam, he has been fretful and unable to sleep for more than a short time. No one can understand what grieves this little one so. Sak Ayi'in, do you remember what our aunts did to soothe the cries of our tiniest family members?"

"I don't know, Chanil. I was too busy playing to notice my cousins until they were old enough to play with me," she said over the baby's wails.

Just then, they both heard an enchanting sound. Apparently little Chan Kayum heard it as well, for his dark almond eyes grew wide as his mouth relaxed shut. It seemed as if he was holding his breath to keep quiet. Coming from the hallway, where Chukah Nuk T'zi always stood at attention, was the sweetest flute music anyone had ever heard. The simple tune with its haunting melody at once satisfied Chan Kayum's hungry mind, just as his thirst was satisfied at his mother's breast.

The two sisters ran to the doorway and observed Chukah playing a blue and red bird-shaped ceramic flute. As his bulky fingers alternately paused over the holes in the top of the flute, the women looked at one another and simultaneously proclaimed, "The *Chilan!*" and burst into laughter.

"If what she said about the baby loving music is true, then my prayers to Ix Chel will be answered, and I will marry and have a baby of my own," giggled Sak Ayi'in. "I wonder who the lucky father will be."

Handing her now sleeping infant to his nursemaid, Chanil walked to the center patio with her sister. "You have your choice of sons from the noble clans here in Palenque. I hope you choose to marry and live here, Sak—although you certainly can journey back to Tikal, if you wish, to marry and raise your family there." The queen watched her sister for the real truth in her eyes, not just her words. This was the first time Chanil had seriously broached the subject of marriage with her sister. She knew Sak Ayi'in's life was full in Palenque, but was constantly aware her older sister had put her desires for marriage and children aside until Chanil's family was established.

"I want to live here in Palenque and watch our children grow up together," Sak Ayi'in said simply.

"The army captain, Keh Cahal, is very handsome, don't you think?" the queen quietly prodded her sister.

"Oh yes! He is handsome and very brave, but I want a man who will be home to share the work with me," Sak Ayi'in said earnestly.

"What work?" said Chanil. "Our life is much better here than it was in Tikal."

"I plan to have six children, and I won't have enough servants to watch them all for me!" Sak Ayi'in laughed again as the two sisters enjoyed the quiet time together.

Later, as Chanil rushed back to her new baby and already leaking milk through her clothing, she encountered Chukah at the nursery door.

"Thank you for your music. It soothed little Chan Kayum—and the rest of us, for that matter. Please play often, Chukah." She smiled at him as she sought out her infant and the relief his suckling brought.

After that, Chukah's flute music filled the palace. Queen Chanil told him she was happy knowing that when Chan Kayum slept, the private hallways were treated to soothing flute music. When the baby was awake or playing, the giant played music that was lighter and caused the servants to dance about as they worked. Gradually, other musicians, who played ceramic and wooden horns and flutes, drums, rattles, and conch shells, joined in the music-making so that the two royal brothers were often entertained by music.

Chukah was glad to serve the royal family and the children in this way. As he played softly, he thought of the beautiful queen and her two children, of the benevolent king who trusted him, and of the dark priest who had saved him from death. He knew that Ah Kan Mai would force him into some intrigue soon—why else would the priest have brought him there? The giant man felt trapped in a web spun by the priest. He and the king's family were all insects stuck there waiting for the inevitable.

CHAPTER TWENTY-THREE

King Akal observed the gathering as he sat in council with Keh Cahal and his four top soldiers. Ah Kan Mai represented the priesthood, as they, Itz'At, and various city elders gathered in the *Popol Na,* the open court beneath the observatory tower. Some were seated on the steps surrounding the courtyard, and others stood facing the king on his outdoor throne. The noblemen were dressed in their most impressive clothing. Some wore turbans of linen, others headdresses of feathers, and all wore dark brown body paint as a contrast to their clothing, but also to ward off the biting flies. They were in heated debate over the advisability of another war—this time with Toniná.

Tilot, the eldest and highest-respected *sahal,* was dressed in his finest and most cumbersome attire of a feathered headdress, peccary tooth necklace, and brightly woven skirts. He stomped his palm wood staff loudly on his stone bench. "Your Majesty! I speak for the other heads of the noble clan families in beseeching you to prepare our troops for war with the mountain kingdom of Toniná. None of us can forget one of the saddest moments in Palenque's history—when Toniná's king captured our revered King Pakal's second son, Kan Hoy Chitan II. Since that day, they have threatened to conquer us and destroy our way of life—our very existence. It is said their custom is to feed on the bodies of their captives!"

A chorus of shouts went up, and a few men murmured to one another, remembering the fearful childhood stories of the *Lo'K'in,* the mythical cannibal survivors of the age of Wooden Men. "Our ancient stories tell how they are covered with green warts and hide in the forest waiting for unsuspecting travelers," said an older *sahal*.

"What if the soldiers of Toniná have been bewitched by their *x'mans* and can change their skin at will?" added another.

"Stop your childish talk!" shouted Tilot. "That rogue city is now reeling from an attack by Calakmul. Toniná's army is not prepared to defend the city from another one. Now is the time! Our grain stores are rapidly depleting, and the many sacrifices to *Cha'ac* are not pleasing him as we had all hoped. Palenque needs more slaves for sacrifice to our rain god." Shouts arose in accord as the king nodded in agreement.

"And may I add, Your Majesty, my family is growing, as are all the *sahal* families. Although our *kayuks* run up the river daily, they do not carry enough food in trade to feed our burgeoning city. We are in desperate need of slaves to clear the rain forest, to make more land available for crops—not to mention our great need for more manpower to continue our city's growth with more temples." Having spoken, Tilot bowed with a flourish, sat down cross-legged on his bench, and slapped his thigh as a final gesture.

King Akal Balam stood and pounded his double-headed snake scepter on the seat. A hush fell over the courtyard. Taking his time, he gazed out at each member of the council and then up and around at the beautiful palace buildings that encircled them all.

After a long silence, he spoke. "I have the supreme gift of having lived in Palenque all my life. It was the wish of the gods I rule over my city for the past ten *tuns* after the reign of the great Wak Kimi Pakal. If my city is threatened, I will defend her. You say Palenque suffers from the threat of outside violence, but we suffer from a far greater foe. An enemy within our walls is slowly attacking our community. Hunger and a loss of morale are working together to bring us down.

"Tilot, my family is growing as well. My heirs to the throne of Palenque will not go hungry. All of you believe a war with Toniná will stop our enemy in its tracks. I have heard reports they are threatening once more to refuse to pay us the tribute we are due. Apparently, my last visit there did not fully convince them of their duty to Palenque. If the council is in accord, we will attack as soon as we are ready.

Keh Cahal, how long will you need to ready your troops for the campaign?"

"It will take one *uinal* to prepare our stores with grain and dried food and to repair and replace our weapons, Great Ahau. By then, the forest floor will no longer be too muddy for travel. The road will be dry and hard and ready for our troops."

"Itz'At," commanded the king to his scribe, "record on your codex that this day was instrumental in the future of Palenque. We prepare for battle with Toniná!"

CHAPTER TWENTY-FOUR

arly the next morning, Keh Cahal admitted to himself he was more than curious about the summons from the queen's servant girl. He didn't know if it was curiosity or just a desire to see Lady Chanil Nab Chel again that made him stride quickly across the courtyard to her rooms. A curt nod was all he allowed acquaintances who were milling about the patios and palace environs. Although he was scheduled to observe the training of his troops, this meeting was first on his agenda. The giant, as always, stood at the doorway to Queen Chanil's suite.

"If you weren't here in the palace guarding the queen and her sons, Chukah, I'd have you winning our wars for us." Keh Cahal smiled as he approached. "Please let Lady Chanil know I am answering her summons." Showing no emotion, but nodding in acknowledgement, the huge servant bowed. Chukah Nuk T'zi's shoulders barely fit through the doorway as he disappeared into the queen's rooms.

"Thank you for coming, Keh Cahal." Chanil stood in the entryway, dwarfed by the giant servant. "It is so warm here in the palace—why don't we sit in the shade of my private courtyard?"

He followed her down a dark hallway that ended at a portal to the dazzling sunshine. Although she was tall for a woman, Queen Chanil Nab Chel was thin and delicate—almost fragile in appearance. Keh Cahal knew her refined features belied a strength he had admired on more than one occasion. He forcefully brushed away the thought of her in his arms in Chinkultic's jungle.

The soldier marveled at how much more beautiful she was today, dressed simply and without the costume of her rank. She sat down on a bench under a large, thorny ceiba tree and beckoned him to sit beside her. Chanil gestured to her serving girl to bring cool drinks and then turned to face him. For a moment, he took in the scene of her seated under their people's most revered tree. Keh Cahal almost believed his queen was as strong as the mythological tree, called *wakahchan,* whose roots reached the gods of the underworld and whose kapok-filled foliage brushed the gods of the heavens.

"I'm still amazed at this exquisite garden, Keh Cahal. The shade of these ceiba and avocado trees brings me peace—especially when I observe tiny birds of every color—and I hear the song of the lovely and tame *k'uk* birds raised here. I know at least *these* birds are safe from the claws of Ah Kan Mai. He'll never kill them just to look for omens in *their* entrails! K'in Balam loves looking for their feathers on the ground and under the plants. It brings me such pleasure when he presents me with these treasures." She smiled at the soldier, and the garden seemed to light up.

"K'in Balam is a born leader, Your Majesty. I enjoy teaching him." Keh Cahal wondered if she had invited him there to speak about birds and babies.

As if reading his mind, she changed the subject. "I understand you will be going to war soon, Keh Cahal. Will Toniná be a formidable enemy?"

"She is a weary and unsuspecting city, Your Majesty, especially since our goodwill visit there recently. We will conquer her this time, but the day will come when Toniná will be a force to reckon with. Ah Kan Mai has our people fearing angry gods who require more and more sacrifices to satisfy them, and Toniná can supply him with many more sacrificial offerings. Are you worried about the king? You must know I am sworn to protect him and would lay down my life for him."

"I have faith the gods are not ready to take either one of you, Keh Cahal." She spoke softly and stirred the cool *posol* corn drink her servant handed her. "My purpose in asking you here was not really to discuss war, but to discuss a more personal subject. Do you remember my sister, Sak Ayi'in?"

"Ah … yes, Your Majesty," he answered guardedly.

"Oh, Keh Cahal," Chanil laughed, sensing his apprehension. "Don't worry, I'm not trying to arrange a marriage for the two of you … but I do want to ask for your help. My sister has expressed an interest in staying here in Palenque to be near her nephews, yet she longs for a family of her own. Can you help me find her a worthy husband? You are acquainted with many more men here than I am. Perhaps when you return from your campaign, you can assist in some introductions."

"It would be my pleasure, Your Majesty." The soldier stood and bowed low.

"Keh Cahal …" Queen Chanil called as he turned to leave. "Thank you for saving my life in Chinkultic. Your bravery not only saved me, but my baby, Prince Chan Kayum. I will never forget that you were there. I feel safe knowing you are here for us. I am aware you must go back to your duties, but I hope to hear from you—if you feel there is a young man suitable for my sister."

He was happy she had chosen to place her confidence in him. "I vow to help you in any way I can," he said, realizing he felt reluctant to walk away from his queen.

CHAPTER TWENTY-FIVE

C ab Men Tun, the king's young architect, knew nothing of the queen's plans. He and Sak Ayi'in fell in love on their own. The conversations between the two had been tentative in the beginning, but grew to genuine friendship as they often walked together after his meetings with the king. Lady Sak frequently expressed to him how she loved to hear about his plans for the king's burial temple as well as his expansion plans for other buildings in the palace. She told him he was her first male confidante, and she could share the things with him she had only shared with her sister before. She also revealed that his calm nature and kind eyes immediately attracted her.

Cab Men Tun was happy to work for the great King Akal. He explained to Sak Ayi'in that since Akal's burial pyramid would take at least five *tuns* to build—even as many as ten *tuns*—the building had already begun. He was proud to be in charge of this great responsibility.

The young architect was a serious young man who coveted a place within the palace walls. His father was a master builder before him whose works had brought beauty to the city of Palenque. Although Lady Sak was not as stunning as her sister, she was pleasant and had a family lineage of which to be proud.

Cab Men Tun decided to speak directly to the king about the marriage before he broached the subject to Lady Sak Ayi'in.

King Akal noticed that young Cab Men Tun was still in the throne room after all the other supplicants had left.

"Is there something you wish to discuss, young man?" Akal asked.

The young architect fell to both knees and spoke. "Oh, Great Ahau, may I be so bold as to present you with a question regarding the queen's sister, Lady Sak Ayi'in?"

Cab Men Tun couldn't see Akal's immediate smile. The king had already guessed the question. He had seen the two walking often with their heads together and laughing.

"What about my wife's sister, young man?" The king enjoyed the architect's discomfort for a moment, not wanting Sak Ayi'in's future husband to take too much for granted just yet.

"I have come to ask you for Sak Ayi'in's hand in marriage." Cab Men Tun looked up earnestly. "We have not discussed it yet, but I have reason to believe she will not turn me down—if I have your permission first, of course, Your Majesty."

"What have you to offer her, Cab Men Tun?" the king asked, trying to look serious. He gestured to the young man to rise and stand before him.

"My family is well-respected here, Great Ahau, and I am building you a temple you will be proud of. Other than that, I have love to offer her and hope for a large family to add to the royal household." Worried that he implied too much, Cab Men Tun quickly bowed low again.

"I cannot speak for Lady Sak Ayi'in, Cab Men Tun. I am sure you are aware her father was killed in battle many years before she and the queen arrived in Palenque, so it is good you came to me first. I will discuss this with her sister. You know I go to war before the next full moon. I am glad you will be here protecting your interests, so to speak, while I am gone. In two days, you will have your answer."

King Akal knew this news would bring happiness to Chanil. In fact, a royal wedding would bring enthusiasm to the whole city and boost morale of the soldiers about to go into battle. Yes, a wedding was a good thing.

The wedding day arrived quickly. The people were excited to have a diversion as notable as a wedding of the queen's sister and one last big celebration before Palenque's soldiers marched off to war.

"You look beautiful, Sak Ayi'in." Chanil fought tears of pride, sweet memories of childhood, and the realization her sister's life was now changing to become everything she had hoped. Chanil helped the attendants with Sak Ayi'in's marriage headdress of feathers and ornaments. "Take this jade pendant to wear for your wedding, as I did for mine," she urged, tying it at her sister's neck.

The noise outside was getting more intense as the people cheered and chanted, anticipating the exciting parade to the temple for the outdoor ceremony. The sisters hugged, and Cab Men Tun came to escort his bride to the Grand Avenue below. He wore a woven tunic of muted yarns over his white *xikul* and an intricately carved headdress accented with quail, turkey, and parrot feathers.

Strangely, Chanil's tears continued to flow. She was grateful for the covered palanquin that hid her from the crowd as she entered the procession. *Why am I so melancholy on a happy day like this? My sister's dreams are finally coming true. Sak Ayi'in is not leaving me; we are welcoming Cab Men Tun into the palace.* Still, Chanil couldn't conquer her feeling of dread.

The night before, Chanil had tried to prepare her sister for the wedding night. Her personal sexual experience was not one of heated bliss as she had hoped for, but she didn't want to disappoint Sak Ayi'in by admitting it.

"Sak, as your married sister, I feel as though we should have a talk about men and marriage. Do you have any wedding night apprehensions?"

"Chanil, you may rest easy and forget your duty to counsel me. Cab Men Tun and I have already experienced the wedding night lovemaking some months ago. I would have told you, but one never knows who is listening. The servants probably already knew our secret when it might have been evident that Cab Men Tun was in the palace very early some mornings." She giggled. "Please don't worry about me, Chanil; I am very happy and will easily and comfortably settle into married life."

With relief, Chanil hugged her sister, wishing Sak Ayi'in every happiness the life of a wife and mother could bring.

At the temple, Queen Chanil and Lady Sak performed the bloodletting ceremony, as did the groom. The people cheered as Men Lamat joined the couple in marriage. When Chanil saw her sister's joyous face, her own unhappy feelings disappeared. She knew her sister's dream had been realized.

Food, *balché,* and dancing were enjoyed by those inside the palace and flowed outside as well, since no one knew for sure how many soldiers would return from Toniná.

"I hate to leave you, Chanil," the king said as he held her tightly on their last night together. "It may be many *uninals* before I return. I feel some comfort in knowing you may depend on Men Lamat's knowledge and Chukah's strength while I am away. I know you don't care for Ah Kan Mai, but he *is* the high priest, and I have his total allegiance. Each campaign is more difficult for this old body. But the thought of you and our sons waiting for me is what brings me home."

"We anxiously await your return, my husband," she whispered as she clung to him and fought her fear of losing him—and the greater fear of her sons growing up without their father. She pressed her head into his chest and remembered her grief at losing her own father on the battlefield.

Chanil prayed silently to Yah'ak Ah for the king's protection. What would happen to her and their boys if Akal were killed in battle? Ah Kan Mai would surely attempt to take over as ruler. The thought made her shiver. Chanil remembered their journey to Toniná and the fearsome palace carvings—blatant warnings to Palenque. They were a warring people, and for the time being, the king had to put them in their place.

She adored Akal; he was her husband and protector, after all. Yet she couldn't help but feel that something was missing when they made love. Although Akal was a gentle and considerate lover, she still needed to use the queen's bath and douche with carefully chosen herbs to soothe her *ch'en* after their laying together. In spite of his gentle touch and unhurried lovemaking, it was still an uncomfortable experience, and she hoped that Sak Ayi'in's loving times with her husband were not as painful as her own. In spite of this she had a full and happy life, and motherhood was her most rewarding job.

Yet why do I find myself thinking about another? Chanil wondered. *Yah'ak Ah, I pray you will protect my husband … and Keh Cahal.*

CHAPTER TWENTY-SIX

The following morning, Men Lamat happily took K'in Balam to see the soldiers before they marched off to Toniná.

"I am going to be Palenque's strongest soldier!" K'in Balam ran and hopped with Men Lamat to the Grand Avenue. He raced ahead, begging the old man to walk faster to where the soldiers were lining up.

"I believe you will be, Little Sprout!" Men Lamat watched the young prince jab and parry with his wooden sword. They approached the hundreds of young men awaiting orders. The soldiers' excitement and anticipation was palpable in the air around them.

"So you want to be a soldier, Little Sprout?"

"Oh, yes, Great Uncle! My father and Keh Cahal have taken me to where the soldiers train. They are very brave and strong!"

"Then you have seen how our troops all live together and are trained in the arts of war from a young age. If you have not seen them prepare for war, I can explain that part to you." Men Lamat saw total admiration in the boy's eyes. "There is no shortage of young men to join the ranks of soldiers. They are cheered and adored by all—and especially by the women." The old man winked at his young charge.

"They begin at dawn with a cup of *posol* and then practice at battle games for the remainder of the day with leather-wrapped obsidian clubs and leather shields. Some are expert at flint and obsidian-edged spears, while others shoot reed arrows with flint tips attached by hemp fibers."

"Yes, Great Uncle. Keh Cahal has been teaching me how to shoot with a bow and arrows!"

"Some soldiers throw darts with a wooden and leather sling. You can recognize the spear-throwers wearing wooden or leather helmets and chest plates. They are just slightly more protected than the young foot soldiers—the *holcans*—who boast only pine-soot blackened tattoos and black body paint instead of armor. Chances are you won't be in this division, but you must know how these men are trained."

"Who are those men, Great Uncle? I like how they are dressed!" The child pointed with his wooden sword to a large group of soldiers standing at attention near them.

"They are Keh Cahal's elite guard. You will be trained as one of these soldiers. They are the most protected in battle. They always wear thick quilted cotton or palm fiber armor covered in deer hide, called *ichca huipil,* as well as helmets and chest plates. Can you see how they carry hatchets and flexible shields decorated with the face of the jaguar god and trimmed with eagle and owl feathers? Their war costumes are topped with jaguar pelts tied to their waists, and stuffed snake skins dangle from their belts, embodying the essence of the serpent for battle. Can you distinguish the various warriors, Little Sprout?"

The boy silently shook his head in acknowledgment, and the wonder in his eyes shone as bright as the soldiers' spearheads.

"The young warriors pray fervently over their flint weapons. The god K'awiil has sent this hard black rock to earth with each lightning strike and buried it in the limestone. They pray he will ensure a victory to those soldiers with the mightiest prayers."

"What is that dangling from this soldier's belt?" The boy's eyes were huge, already anticipating the answer as he pointed to a nearby warrior.

"These young men wear the dried jawbones of their victims as trophies on their belts to intimidate the enemy." K'in Balam grew serious as he poked at the human jawbone swinging from the soldier's belt.

"Do you see the older men over there, also getting ready to march?" said Men Lamat.

"Do they fight, too?" K'in Balam looked perplexed.

"No, my boy. They have long ago lost their strength for fighting, so they play the leather-topped *tax* war drums made from hollowed logs or blow the *hom tas*—the long wooden trumpets of battle.

"At night, most of the young soldiers play the war board game, *Bol,* until dawn or add to the impressive artwork of tattoos on their bodies.

"Since time began, warriors' women are never far away—preparing food, mending clothing, applying medicinal herbs, and bringing comfort to their men. Only the experienced older soldiers have the sense to at least get *some* sleep!" The old teacher laughed in spite of the knowledge that many of the men before him would never see Palenque again.

He continued his lesson on the soldier's life. "At dawn, these young men's spirits are still high from last night's dancing the *holcan-okot,* or warriors' dance, during which they have taken turns wearing the jaguar skin to absorb the strength and magical powers of the revered big cat. To fortify their resolve, I am sure they all drank as many goblets of *balché* as they could hold."

"I see the king! He is the grandest man in the whole army!" The boy jumped up and down, trying to get a better look at his father. "Is he going to do the blood ceremony now? The gods will surely grant Palenque victory after my father prays."

"Yes. See your father drawing blood in prayer to the gods? Look how all ranks of soldiers stand at attention. Now let's listen to the rousing speech about to begin by their commander, Keh Cahal."

"Warriors of Palenque!" The king's general strode up and down the flanks of eager young men who were prepared to battle the enemy for their king. "Today, we will march toward Toniná. Before the next full moon, we will rejoice at their king's sacrifice here in Palenque! King Akal will clasp him by his hair and proclaim him Palenque's captive! We will all see his humiliation as his hands are tied and he is stripped of his finery to only his loincloth and paper rolls replace his royal jade earplugs. We are stronger than they are, our troops are better equipped, and the gods are on the side of Palenque!"

"Pa-len-que! Pa-len-que!" The soldiers shouted in unison, and the beating of drums concurred.

"Our great king, Akal Balam," Keh Cahal continued, "has performed his holy ceremony in front of all of you. He has spoken to the gods, who assured him we will be victorious! When we return home to Palenque, Toniná's king will be led behind our bravest soldiers in a parade to the sacrificial stone. Toniná's captured soldiers will carry its many treasures to Palenque, and we will dine on feasts prepared by our grateful women—who will indeed show you how grateful they are that night!"

"My girlfriend is already grateful!" one soldier shouted.

"You're right!" yelled another. "She showed *me* how grateful she was while you were busy getting drunk!" Boisterous laughing began.

Keh Cahal raised his hand to silence them. "If you do not return to Palenque, the gods shall reward you in *Xibalbá*. From the heavens, you will witness the glory of Palenque and know it was your sacrifice that made it so!" His eyes swept the crowd, and then he placed his leather *ko'haw* on his head and proclaimed, "*Ko'ox!* We march!"

The drums began a slow beat, the trumpets sounded, and the soldiers set off on their ten-day march to the enemy capital. Families lined the road, throwing flowers and shouting encouragement to the soldiers—young and old.

Queen Chanil watched from the palace. She could see her uncle Men Lamat, joined by Sak Ayi'in, who held tight to the tug of K'in Balam's hand, down at the front of the palace on the Grand Avenue. The boy strained to run to his father as the king marched by, taller than any man in the army. But Lady Sak held him securely. Chanil smiled as she watched her sister's natural maternal gestures. Lady Sak hugged her nephew and pointed to the soldiers. She laughed at something the boy said and then kissed his cheek.

Chanil was delighted her sister had found peace and happiness with a husband who would be by her side, just as she had hoped. Perhaps a baby would come soon to complete Sak Ayi'in's life.

CHAPTER TWENTY-SEVEN

AD 876

Men Lamat entered the *Itzám Nah*—the sacred underground house of the priests. In one of Palenque's most holy of rooms, known as the *kunul,* or conjuring place, the priests converged to drink balché, smoke their hallucinogen-laced cigars, and perform ritualistic enemas. No women were ever allowed in this holy place. Their essence would contaminate the room and anger the gods. The men gathered to share their knowledge of vision-inducing liquids and powders and to trade obsidian blades for cutting and piercing.

Men Lamat was well aware that Ah Kan Mai typically held court, keeping the other *x'mans* at a distance. The lower priests' camaraderie was evident, as was the high priest's aloof and imperious air.

"Welcome, Men Lamat." A young priest bowed to the old man's status. The conversation faded to whispers as Men Lamat entered the darkened room. He uttered greetings to several priests and then saw Ah Kan Mai. The old priest simply nodded to him and turned his back on the high priest to sit cross-legged on a woven mat on the floor, joining a group of other priests.

All in attendance noticed the affront to the high priest. Almost immediately, Men Lamat heard the ominous tinkling of shells and then sensed a shadow darkening the light of the wall torch behind him. He felt the presence of Ah Kan Mai standing there.

"I find it intriguing that you have finally decided to visit the priests' house, Men Lamat."

The old man's strong legs raised his body without too much difficulty as he stood and turned to face Ah Kan Mai, whose lips were smiling, but whose eyes were as cold as the grim and frightful faces of the deities painted on the walls.

"My first duties are to the queen and her sons, Ah Kan Mai. Although I have spent many years with Tikal's priests, I believe one can always learn new things. Perhaps I will learn something here tonight—or it is possible I will teach something new to *someone else*." The older priest locked eyes with Ah Kan Mai.

"Well then, show us what is taught to your *x'mans* in Tikal." The high priest's voice sounded like more of a warning than an invitation.

Men Lamat sat quietly again and closed his eyes in deep concentration for a few moments. Suddenly, the frail man's voice bellowed out as loud as the army's war horns as he called forth his personal gods to assist him. With eyes still closed, he extended his arms over the earthen floor in front of him, and a small fire began to burn on the bare dirt, appearing to feed only on the energy from Men Lamat's hands. The fire grew as it roared and sucked on the air.

Whispered murmurs began among the priests. "How can he do this?" "Can he control the fire?"

As the threatening flames grew to the height of half a man, a wind started to stir within the center of the room. It began to swirl and howl in a circular motion and narrow its spiral above the fire—as though the god Huracan himself was there.

Men Lamat opened his eyes to look up at Ah Kan Mai. The high priest's arms were high in the air, directing the wind he had created to swirl down and extinguish Men Lamat's magical fire. Just before the great wind blew out the wall torches, Men Lamat's eyes rolled back into his head, and he opened his mouth to emit a terrifying and piercing howl that drove everyone out of the room, including Ah Kan Mai.

Men Lamat arose slowly and began to walk back to his rooms. He heard a few priests discussing the scene in the *Itzám Nah*.

"The fearsome sound was a combination of a dying jaguar and a hungry eagle—certainly not a sound that could be produced by an old man," one priest declared.

"We all are puzzled at how a sound could stop a small hurricane, but we were there and can verify what we saw."

"Look how Men Lamat walks calmly out of the mat house with smoke still clinging to his robes!" They continued describing the experience as they huddled, unaware of the old man's ability to hear them.

The aged priest returned to his rooms and fell into a deep sleep, weary to his bones. That bit of magic took almost all of his strength, but he was confident he had shown the high priest he was still a force with which to be reckoned.

Ah Kan Mai walked slowly back to his tower. Men Lamat had proved he was well schooled. The high priest had seen the fire magic before, but the sound the old man produced had taken him aback. Men Lamat could get in the way of his plans, after all. Saving Palenque from intruders had become slightly more difficult.

Ah Kan Mai smiled; he liked a challenge.

CHAPTER TWENTY-EIGHT

K'in Balam didn't know why he had to be in the hot and semi-darkened room under the tower with Ah Kan Mai. This skinny old priest with frightening eyes wasn't his teacher—kind Great-Uncle Men Lamat was. When a lower priest had come to get the boy, Queen Chanil seemed too preoccupied with his baby brother to notice his exit. The young prince couldn't complain to his father or to Keh Cahal, as they were at war far away in Toniná. K'in Balam didn't want to cry to his mother; she would think he was a baby and not a grown-up boy of five *tuns*. Besides, she was busy with his little brother now anyway, and only *he* was asked to this important meeting—not anyone else. K'in Balam would listen to what this man who smelled bad would say and then decide what he would tell his mother.

"It will be many *tuns* before you become king, K'in Balam, but your mother has reminded me that it is about time to begin your lessons concerning kingship. I will reveal many secrets to you that are not for women's ears, so I hope you are grown-up enough to keep these secrets.

"You will be expected to nourish the gods with your gift of blood, as is your duty, for a king's blood is the most sacred substance one can give the gods. You are not yet ready to perform the blood sacrifice, but when the time comes, I will teach you how to pierce your little *yat* and how to endure the pain of this holy procedure.

"You, of course, will then take a captive in battle and sacrifice your victim in a very holy ceremony at your accession rites, or you will not be ready—or worthy—to hold an office as great as king. I will teach you how to communicate with the gods on behalf of your people and show you how to lead Palenque in the *right* direction."

Ah Kan Mai seemed to go on and on about *this* sacrifice and *that* ceremony, and K'in Balam's head just couldn't hold any more. He was beginning to squirm on the hard limestone bench where he had been told to sit. All this talk about his *yat* made him have to relieve himself.

"Be still, my Little Sprout; I have much to teach you. Obviously, the first lesson is to be about self-control," the priest said as he bent down and brought his hooked nose close to K'in Balam's face. *Ah Kan Mai smells of stinky food and pee,* the little boy thought.

"I have much to teach you while your father is away at war and while your mother is more concerned with your little brother.

"All Maya kings and priests hold secret knowledge, and it is our duty to keep these skills alive and to ourselves. If our mysteries are dispersed to the ignorant peasants, they would not know how to use the command of magic and potions." He paused to allow what he had said to be absorbed by his young pupil.

"Our teachings are on codices kept here in the palace, but they may not be as safe as I would like. As many of our gods reside in the caves of the mountains that protect us, I plan to have our precious records and books moved to a secret location only the gods and I will know. When you are king, you will need *me* to reveal to you just where they are. Remember that, K'in Balam. The success of your reign in Palenque will depend on it!"

Little K'in Balam could not hold his body's natural functions any longer and he didn't know what else to do, so he let himself pee just where he sat. Hearing the sound of liquid splashing to the floor caused the priest to stop his lecture and glare at his pupil. The boy had nothing to say and hung his head in shame, trying to avoid the frightful stare of his new teacher.

Imperiously scrutinizing his royal charge, Ah Kan Mai sighed and declared, "Perhaps it is premature and you are too young to begin your lessons, K'in Balam. When your mother asks me again about your education, I will inform her you are not yet ready. You can trust me not to tell her you peed in your clothes, just as your tiny brother does. I am sure you would not want to be a disappointment to her." With a sigh, he added, "You probably haven't listened to a word I said.

"You may return to your toys now, Little Sprout, but we will meet again when the time is right for serious teaching. You must understand now that I will be your principal teacher, and that Men Lamat will be out of the palace soon. You may leave now."

K'in Balam fled across the courtyard, his sandaled feet running atop the carved limestone Walkway of the Shamed Warriors. It was fitting that it depicted the nine shamed captives of the Great Pakal, hands tied behind them and ankles bound, awaiting their doom. Dodging the workers, Chukah, and his mother's maids, he finally reached his room, hoping no one could see he had soiled his wrapped skirt and undergarments. He buried his face in the soft blankets of his pallet and tried to hide his tears of disgrace. The little boy decided he couldn't tell his mother or Great-Uncle Men Lamat. K'in Balam wouldn't think about what had just happened; he knew how to keep a secret.

CHAPTER TWENTY-NINE

Some of Men Lamat's happiest times were with his niece, Chanil, and her children. As he approached the queen's rooms, he smiled as he watched little Chan Kayum sitting on the floor opposite Chukah, who sat cross-legged, showing the boy how to play a song on the ceramic flute.

"You are a good teacher, Chukah. The boy seems to have a real talent for music, and you are his inspiration. But for now, he needs to run and play outside. We mustn't let him spend too much time sitting inside. In fact, I am going to follow my own advice." Men Lamat stopped to pat the little boy on the head. "Chan Kayum, come with me to get your brother. Let's go out to the grassy courtyard near my rooms, and you can play your flute for your proud mother."

"Uncle Men Lamat, I love this special time with you and my sons as they play here." The young queen took her uncle's hand in hers as they approached the quiet patio. "Because trees and buildings shade this courtyard, the air here is usually cooler than elsewhere on the palace grounds."

"Mama, listen to what Chukah taught me today. I learned to play this song to make the giant fireflies dance!" Chan Kayum began a beautiful melody employing sweet high notes and lower rich tones.

"I'm sure your music will make them shine even more brilliantly, my son." Chanil smiled at her youngest boy.

"Now play loud music as I march toward the enemy!" K'in Balam shouted, and he began marching toward a tree.

Chanil and Men Lamat laughed and sat on an intricately carved stone bench. "See how little Chan Kayum particularly likes playing his flute for K'in Balam?" the queen said. "It is evident through Chukah's patient lessons, the child has learned to play with heartfelt emotion. The sounds he produces can make his nursemaids happy or bring them to tears!"

"Yes, my sweet Chanil. Since K'in Balam is often busy with lessons, little Chan Kayum spends much of his time in the company of the palace women and his flute teacher, Chukah. The little one's skill with the ceramic flute has surprised everyone. He can even mimic the sounds of the birds of the jungle.

"The vibrations of music can heal the body as well as the soul. I like seeing how Chan Kayum's music accompanies his brother's sword practice. Look how the older boy's lunges and sidesteps become a kind of dance," the old teacher said, smiling.

"Play faster, Chan Kayum!" K'in Balam said. "I want to be the fastest and strongest soldier in the army!"

The younger boy marched in circles as he played his ceramic flute, and his brother hopped and lunged, sparring with an imaginary enemy.

"Do you see their strong resemblance, Uncle Men Lamat?" Chanil asked.

"They are surely related. Chan Kayum will probably not reach the height of his older brother. Although he is a head taller than other children his age, his legs and arms are shorter and sturdier than K'in Balam's. Still, he is a true Maya, My Queen."

"The affinity between the two boys is obvious, too. I am happy to see my sons truly like each other as friends and enjoy spending time together. Having a sibling is so very important," added Chanil. "I can't imagine growing up without my sister."

The old priest saw a shadow fall over Chanil's face.

"During the three *uinals* of the king's absence at war, I have noticed how my sister's appearance has changed, Uncle. She has been looking pale and thin. Sak Ayi'in revealed to me she is pregnant. Even though

Sak is excited and happy about it, she is feeling ill and needs to rest often. I miss my sister's company. Ever since her marriage, Sak Ayi'in has been very busy attending to her new husband and redecorating their rooms in preparation for the baby."

"Perhaps she is just exhausted from her new life, dearesr Chanil," assured Men Lamat.

"I feel something is wrong with Sak Ayi'in," said Chanil. "Tomorrow I shall seek her out, and we will have the good heart-to-heart talk long overdue. I expect her smile to wash my worries away."

"I know it will." The old priest patted Chanil's hand. But at the thought of Lady Sak Ayi'in, Men Lamat felt a gnawing at the pit of his stomach. Even he had noticed the hollows under his older niece's eyes. He would pray later. Perhaps the gods would provide the answer.

CHAPTER THIRTY

Attracted by happy hoots and shouts, Sak Ayi'in walked to the edge of the water to where three handsome men were laughing and splashing one another.

Are they soldiers? she wondered. *Why aren't they away at war with Toniná?* The men didn't appear to notice her as they splashed and swam near the waterfall of the Queen's Bath. *Why are they here? This particular bath is just for the palace women,* she thought. *How strange! That great splashing seems to come from huge fish tails each time they dive into the water! Oh, Great Ix Chel, protect me ... these men must be the Xoc, the mythical mermen we have been taught to fear since childhood!* Sak Ayi'in stepped behind a nearby tree to hide. Although frightened, she was curious and poked her head out to watch them frolic.

One of them noticed her and alerted the others. They waved and smiled—then played some more. Sak Ayi'in was so tired, she couldn't run away, so she leaned against the tree, compelled to watch them enjoying themselves. One of the men waved to her again and motioned for her to join them. Sak looked at the serene, cool water as it rippled at her feet.

"Come with us!" the same man called out to her. He smiled and splashed, looking young and handsome in the waist-deep water. She remembered the stories about the *Xoc*—how they lured women into the water to pull them to their underwater world.

"No!" Sak Ayi'in called back, "I mustn't ..." She thought of her baby and clutched her small, rounded belly. She was very tired; it was difficult to stay awake. Lady Sak just wanted to lie down somewhere and rest or maybe float on her back and sleep while the current carried her and the baby in her womb to a quiet, cool shore where she could rest under the shade of a tree. She was very hot and thirsty. The cool water would be good to drink.

Sak Ayi'in couldn't help smiling to herself as she watched two of the *Xoc* men playing together, laughing and trying to dunk one another. The third one—and the most handsome—floated toward her, beckoning.

"Just take my hand, and if you cannot swim, I will help you stay afloat right here in the cool water, close to the shore." He smiled and reached for her.

They aren't frightening at all. The stories about them are wrong! He seems so trustworthy. I wonder where Chanil is? I want to tell her I am safe here at the Queen's Bath. This young, handsome man will help me find a place to rest.

His smile was beautiful! She reached for his outstretched left hand. As he clasped her hand firmly, his right arm came up out of the water, holding a spear. Sak Ayi'in saw it glimmer in the dappled sunlight, filtering through the thick trees surrounding the pond.

The spear moved swiftly as he thrust it deep into her belly. The pain took her breath away. Over and over he struck her—again and again!

"Ahhhh!" She screamed in her dream and plunged beneath the cool water. She was drowning in a red lake. *My baby! My baby …*

In the pallet next to him, Cab Men Tun heard Sak Ayi'in cry out. He sat up and saw his young wife lying in a pool of blood.

"My beloved!" the young man cried. He held her and tried to staunch the flow of blood between her legs with the bedclothes.

"The Xoc … they were at the Queen's Bath … his spear …" were the last words Lady Sak Ayi'in uttered before slumping in her new husband's arms. Cab Men Tun called for the servants, who in turn ran for the priests.

"No one, not even the x'*mans*, could save her, my sweet Chanil. She would never have had the baby," Men Lamat said softly as he and Queen Chanil stood over her sister's lifeless body in Sak Ayi'in's chambers. Cab Men Tun was kneeling at the bed and still holding her hand as he wept.

"Her pregnancy was just too precarious from the beginning. At four months, even total bed rest and medicinal teas could not help her keep this child. Perhaps the Rainbow Serpent connecting her to the baby was not strong. It is not for us to know what her future might have been. But she and her baby are together now, and they both have earned the privilege of returning to this world soon."

Queen Chanil was inconsolable. Men Lamat felt his words were inadequate and of no help. The only thing they all could do now was to prepare Lady Sak Ayi'in's funeral.

CHAPTER THIRTY-ONE

"It is regrettable how the Second Wife's pregnant sister died so suddenly." The king's daughter, Lady Yax Koh, paced her room and had to remind herself that no one could trace the poison back to her—and hopefully, not her mother, Lady Zac Ku, who sipped tea at a small table near her. Yax Koh fumed, wondering how many frightening occurrences it would take to make Lady Chanil leave Palenque. Maybe then their lives could return to normal.

"How dare that foreign woman come here to our home, get pregnant twice—and then to make matters worse, her sister becomes pregnant as well. It is just too much to take! I only want what is best for Palenque, Mother. Now it appears I am never going to bear a child of my own. The best successor to the king would be my own husband—not your brother." Her mother, Lady Zac Ku, was getting old as well and seemed to turn over Palenque's future to the intruding whore. Yax Koh didn't mind telling her mother so—and often.

"You must not do anything that will draw attention to you, Yax Koh. There are too many eyes here in the palace. Be very careful about what you may plan," the old queen cautioned.

"I only want what is best for our family, our city, and ultimately the king, Mother—although it appears my father has completely forgotten he has a daughter. Perhaps he remembered when he took a woman younger than I am to his bed! The Second Wife and her entourage are taking over. Her priest, their servants, crying babies … can't Ah Kan Mai do anything to help us?"

"We must let him consult the stars for what is best for the future of Palenque, my daughter. I know it angers you to see the children being born from Lady Chanil and nearly from her sister. Perhaps this is the wish of the gods."

"It can't be! If you won't help me, then I'll figure out a plan of my own!"

Recently, Lady Yax Koh's maid had come to her asking if her sister could work for her and Lady Zac Ku. Once the king's daughter had seen the pretty sister, Mu'ut Ek, she graciously pushed her jealousy aside and began to think how such a comely young woman's gifts could best be used. Yax Koh immediately noticed the young girl's effect on men and vowed to remember that bit of good fortune.

How easily this new servant girl accepts her duties. She quietly delivered the special tea to Lady Sak infused with strong herbs to flush pregnancy from the body. The young Mu'ut Ek is going to be valuable as a quiet and trustworthy asset. Perhaps I'll introduce her to Ah Kan Mai. He'll know how to use her talents!

CHAPTER THIRTY-TWO

AD 878

Palenque's royal scribe, Itz'At, truly was happiest when he could teach his skills to others—and never more so than when he worked with the young prince, K'in Balam.

He saw in K'in Balam a natural curiosity for learning and an ability to grasp the fundamentals of priesthood—as all kings were primarily priests. Yet the young prince was already showing signs of the fearlessness needed for the expected self-sacrificial duties and for combat. Although the king doted on the boy, the young scribe observed that the more active influences on the child came from his old teacher, Men Lamat, and from the king's captain, Keh Cahal.

Itz'At was suspicious of K'in Balam's newest teacher, Ah Kan Mai, whose excessive use of hallucinogenic substances kept him in the other world of fearsome gods much of the time. The scribe was relieved the high priest hadn't yet overly influenced the young prince about these substances and was glad K'in Balam had not yet tried to emulate Ah Kan Mai.

Itz'At had observed the high priest having frequent meetings with the *Puuc* traders, who were known to carry gossip from kingdom to kingdom, stirring up rivalry between the city-states to their own advantage. Their growing influence appeared as stylish trends when local shop owners began wearing mustaches like the foreign traders and the upper class acquired more and more unusual pottery and clothing from other cities. Because they ensured their services by trading secrets for goods, there was no stopping these *Puuc* foreigners. It was not Itz'At's place to speak to the king about his suspicions.

Although King Akal had a successful campaign against Toniná, the victory celebrations had lost their luster. Akal had taken their king prisoner, rather than executing him, and torture of a few captives did little to appease the populace. The king appeared more short-tempered lately. Itz'At felt he could at least express his concerns with Men Lamat. He found the old teacher in his rooms, studying a pile of codices.

"K'in Balam tells me he is preparing for his designation rites, Men Lamat. How will he fare at that grand ceremony?"

"I wish I could tell you I have been the one guiding him in this, but when he reached the age of six *tuns,* Ah Kan Mai began the boy's exclusive training. As you know, we gather for the event at the next full moon. I can only hope all I have taught him up to this point has been a sturdy foundation for the inevitable lessons in fear and magic Ah Kan Mai has in store."

"I have seen Ah Kan Mai with the *Puuc* traders. Do you suppose he trades Palenque's wealth for his potions?" the scribe asked carefully.

"I do not know what he is up to, but I wouldn't be surprised if he is trading our treasures in exchange for stories of fear and rebellion from the other cities in our region. It is best Palenque's people don't find out too much about the uprisings and sackings of major palaces like Dos Pilas and Aquateca. Gossip spreads like a disease, and we do not need to add that to our city's problems. It is best we focus on the celebration of K'in Balam's coming designation rites."

K'in Balam was ready. He was well prepared for the special night of the full moon. The boy stood with his parents at the foot of the palace as the grand procession headed by Ah Kan Mai stopped before them. They joined in behind the high priest, and a cadre of priests followed them as they headed up the main avenue to the Great Temple. The people lined the wide street and cheered K'in Balam, who wore the serious expression of a prince undertaking the awesome training of kingship.

K'in Balam, at six *tuns,* was proud that he was already taller than most boys two *tuns* older than he.

Inside the temple, torches threw dancing shadows along the walls. Censers lining the edge of the throne platform burned copal incense, filling the room with pungent, pine-scented smoke. Itz'At sat at the feet of Akal's throne with his pots and paintbrushes, detailing the special ceremony in his books.

K'in Balam sat in the center of the room as his father chanted and danced the touching and solemn centuries-old *ak'ot ahau,* the ritual dance performed by kings for their sons. As the drums beat a slow and steady rhythm, the king danced the history of the great Hun Hunahpu, the Corn God. In a dramatic pantomime, he struck the holy mountain open to reveal corn to the world. He danced the creation of man from the corn and the blood of the gods. Finally, he danced the ceremonial handing of the revered scepter of kingship to his son.

"Someday, you will also be called Holy Lord of Palenque, my son." With a heavy sigh, the king ended the dance and knelt in supplication to the gods.

Leaning laboriously on his staff, he arose and sat cross-legged on his throne. In awed silence, Palenque's inner circle of priests bowed to their king. Ah Kan Mai nodded to K'in Balam, who stood as his servants helped him strip down to only his *ex.* This white undergarment was made of a long swatch of linen edged in his mother's fine handiwork of shells and pearls and carefully wrapped around his loins. It was tied so the ends hung down in front and in back.

The barefoot boy strode confidently forward to his mother, who wore her most elegant costume of office and sat emotionless to the left of the king. K'in Balam bowed to her. He then turned to his father and knelt, touching his head to the floor, extending his arms forward. The young prince arose, bowed, and lit the fragrant *pom* in the white censer to acknowledge the north direction. He repeated the procedure with the red censer for the east, the yellow for the south, and the black for the west.

As the six under-priests beat their drums and chanted their sacred combinations of sounds, K'in Balam then approached Ah Kan Mai and accepted the ritual cigar handed to him. Its heady aroma made the boy's mind spin as he was led to a stone bench, and he felt himself succumb to the drug imbedded in its leaves.

The boy then clearly saw a vision of a young corn plant growing in the nurturing soil of Palenque. He felt his own body become tall and straight as the corn stalk. His arms swayed in the breeze as they turned into the long, graceful leaves of the corn plant. K'in Balam's thick, dark hair, which had been tied up and back in plaits, now became the silky yellow and green threads of the cob, and his head felt full of the sacred kernels as they grew. He saw himself in a huge cornfield with immature corn plants growing as far as the eye could see.

Then the boy saw workers violently cutting down young neighboring corn plants and setting the large piles of new corn ablaze. *Stop!* he tried to tell them. *You cannot burn us yet! We aren't ready—our heads of corn must be cut first to feed the people!* But they wouldn't hear his pleas. The peasants kept coming closer and closer with their stone hatchets to cut away at the life of the corn.

K'in Balam felt searing pain through the skin of his scrotum and became alert to the ceremony once again. He hoped he hadn't flinched as Ah Kan Mai pierced his *yat* for the royal blood. He wanted to look to his mother for reassurance but knew she could not meet his stare. The boy stood and closed his eyes to the pain as his blood was captured in the high priest's *lac*.

After the piercing, as his blood burned, mixing with the smoke of the wall torches and censors, he prayed aloud to Itzamná for the blessing befitting the son of a king. And as he was taught, he thanked the gods for the gift of his teacher, Ah Kan Mai. Silently, he hoped it would soon be over.

K'in Balam's next significant ceremony would come when he sacrificed a captive he would have to take in battle. Only then would the young prince be sanctified to rule. But that would be many *tuns* in the future. Now, he just wanted to be near his mother and watch the grand celebration soon to begin. But for the moment, the boy had to remain there as a brave young prince and only pretend his mother was holding his hand.

He stood straight with his most regal expression. *Perhaps after the ceremonies, I will be allowed to visit Great-Uncle Men Lamat and ask him what my vision meant.*

CHAPTER THIRTY-THREE

AD 878

"The people are afraid, Your Majesty. There is talk in the villages of great, dark clouds of locusts that have fed on the corn of several cities to the south. That is not all, Great *Ahau*. We have heard how fierce hurricanes are decimating the land to the southeast, while we are suffering yet another year of scant rain. They say the gods are punishing us and sending dire warnings. The people say the gods are displeased with us and may send another flood to destroy us, as they did to the race of wooden men ..." The emissary from Tikal, kneeling at the foot of Akal's throne, paused to take a breath and to remove his broad, circular white ambassador's hat.

"Now, calm down, Nik Te Mu," the king said, noticing the *ebet* from Tikal had not yet removed his outer traveling cloak of white linen edged in shells. This cloak was a symbol of immunity, even in war. "Take a breath, and tell me—who are *they?*" Akal concealed his alarm from this messenger of King K'awiil of Tikal. "Someone get this man a cup of *balché* to calm his nerves!"

Urgent whispers began among the priests and *sahals* from the neighboring villages who stood at the sides of the throne room. King Akal hadn't been home one *uinal* since his victorious return from Toniná when the persistent rumors began cropping up on a daily basis.

Accepting a cup of the strong bark drink himself, King Akal prodded the man once more. "Who are *they?*"

"The *Puuc* traders, oh Great *Ahau,*" the kneeling man finally revealed. "They travel throughout the Maya lands on the waterways by *kayuks* and roads. They hear and see many things. These traders say the gods are displeased and are going to punish us all! I have heard them saying the gods are blaming the *kings,* and the poor people are going to suffer even more than they do now." Exhausted, he bowed his head to the floor.

King Akal was quiet for a moment. He knew the purveyors of damaging gossip were many, and they traveled throughout the entire region, spreading the fungus of fear and distrust. These militaristic traders, who used slaves to carry the heavy goods between the cities, traveled by canoe from city to city, spreading news and gossip. The king now realized these warrior merchants had become much too powerful in the delicate balance of commerce between the city-states.

"After you have eaten and rested, go back to Tikal and tell King Hasau Chan K'awiil I desire a council between us. Tikal has thirteen provinces, and its king may be having trouble keeping those *tzuks* free of gossipers. We taught our wayward *tzuk,* Toniná, a lesson she won't soon forget. It is time we deal with the *Puuc* as well. Ask Tikal's king to journey here, and within the walls of Palenque, we will decide how to quell these rumors once and for all!"

Akal unfolded his legs and stood next to the carved jaguar-headed throne. His dark eyes grew ominously calm as he addressed the ministers, priests, and all in attendance. "If I hear of *anyone* in Palenque spreading these lies, he will find himself on the *chac-chac* platform, and his fresh heart a meal for the gods!" The king strode from the temple knowing well the fear he left behind.

Itz'At hurriedly put his quills and paints away, folded his codices, and knew he must relate to Men Lamat what had just taken place. He walked to the queen's section of the palace and took the steps heading down to her priest's simple quarters. The scribe had been concerned about the old priest lately. Since the queen's sister's death, Men Lamat had aged a great deal—and much too quickly.

"I had a dream that Yum Chom, lord of the vultures, was in search of me." Men Lamat spoke softly from a chair in his darkened room. "So, in my dream, I stopped hiding and allowed him to find me. He awaits my death. Sometimes—in my wakened state—I see a spirit *cib* crouched in the tree outside, patiently waiting for me to die so he might feast on my flesh."

Alarmed, Itz'At rushed to the frail man. "But you must not allow this dream to control your destiny. The queen and her children need you here. You will leave her defenseless against Ah Kan Mai!"

"We have no control over our destiny, my son," Men Lamat said calmly. "The gods use us as they need, and we die too soon. We can only hope to reincarnate to a better life."

"The king has called for a counsel with Tikal's king. They will discuss the rumors of many cities falling to the peasants. I thought you would want to know, Men Lamat," the young scribe said.

"I will be alive when the Council of Kings convenes. Queen Chanil's aunt, Lady Twelve Macaw of Tikal, will travel here with my brother, the king, and will be good company for Chanil. Our queen has not seen her relatives since her marriage seven *tuns* past. Ah Kan Mai will not disrupt anything while we have royal visitors. Do not worry that I will journey to *Xibalbá* this *uinal,* my son. But it will be soon enough. I will rest now."

Reluctantly, Itz'At left the old priest and wondered what would become of Queen Chanil and her two children during the next inevitable campaign against Palenque's enemies.

The young scribe was happy he and the queen and had become closer friends since he began to teach K'in Balam. In his conversations with her, the scribe could see how much she truly cared for the people and how attentive she was to the palace activities around her. How could *he* defend his queen? Itz'At despised his own frail body and small stature.

He knew his queen did not like Ah Kan Mai any more than the high priest liked her. Perhaps there was another way to fight the influential man. Those closest to the queen had to be made to understand they could help. Perhaps her huge servant could be an ally. He decided to speak with Chukah Nuk T'zi, who stood outside the queen's rooms. It was a good time to talk to him; Itz'At knew that Chanil and the children were with the king.

"Hello, Chukah. I thought I might discuss with you some concerns I have regarding the queen and her sons." The giant bowed and looked at the small young man. "I know the high priest brought you to the palace, so perhaps your allegiance to him is greater than yours to Queen Chanil. But may I just caution you that she and her sons need your protection now more than ever." Itz'At was sure he saw a look of concern in the giant's eyes.

"Rumors are rampant about unrest in other cities, so it is possible the king will leave again on another campaign. The queen will need those of us who remain in the palace at that time to be even more vigilant in our protection of her and Palenque's princes. That won't be until after the Council of Kings meeting, which is to be held here soon. The queen's uncle, the king of Tikal, will be happy to know you are guarding his beloved niece and her children. But after the visitors leave, Queen Chanil will need even more watchful eyes protecting her." Chukah nodded his head in understanding.

"Her uncle is not in good health. His magic can only help to defend her while he is strong enough to do so. As you can see, I am not strong, but I am smart. Chukah, the gods have blessed you with strength and intelligence. I pray you will never have to use your gifts in defense of our queen.

"I hear the queen returning with the boys. The sound of Chan Kayum's flute is unmistakable. I will leave you to reflect on my words."

With that, Itz'At left the giant. The scribe vowed to be even more observant of his surroundings. If his own talents could protect Queen Chanil, he would find a way.

CHAPTER THIRTY-FOUR

"Mama, please tell the story again," Chan Kayum pleaded. "The part about the Four Hundred Boys!"

Chanil loved this time with her sons. "I will tell you the story, and then you must rest. Sleep will make you big and strong enough to keep up with your older brother." Chanil smiled and sat on Chan Kayum's pallet to retell his favorite part of the Maya history. Her boys settled under their covers.

"Well, it seems that Zipacna, the oldest son of Seven Macaw, was going around bragging he was the maker of mountains," she began. "He came upon the Four Hundred Boys, who were having a hard time trying to drag a heavy log to use for a beam of a house they were building. 'What are you boys doing?' he asked.

"When they explained, he offered to help and carried the log all by himself to the location they pointed out. Secretly agreeing that he was much too strong and could be a threat to them, the Four Hundred Boys decided to have him dig a hole for the pole, and then they would attack him and throw him under the pole when he wasn't looking. But Zipacna was sneaky and had heard them planning his death. He dug and dug very deeply for the cavity they asked for, all the while assuring them he was close to being finished. But this trickster was digging two holes! He made a second one connected by a tunnel to the first opening for his own safe hiding place.

"'I am finished,' he called out at last to the Four Hundred Boys from the first hole in the ground. And they quickly threw the pole standing upright in the hole to bury him!'"

"Then what happened, Mama?" Chan Kayum's eyes were huge in anticipation of the rest of the story.

"Zipacna immediately started chewing off some of his hair and fingernails to give to the busy ants to bring up and eat at the surface of the earth.

"'Look,' cried the Four Hundred Boys, 'the ants are eating Zipacna! Now he is finished and will no longer be a threat to us!'

"While they were rejoicing inside their new house and drinking too much *balché*, Zipacna emerged from his hiding place and knocked the house down on top of them! In death, they flew up to the sky and became the Pleiades, where they appear to be a handful of bright seeds shining down on us. At the time of year when they sink in the Western sky, we know it is time to plant our seeds.

"Now, no more stories tonight, my little ones. I will ask Chukah to play his flute and soothe your busy minds to sleep."

She kissed Chan Kayum and went to cover K'in Balam and kiss him one more time. As she sat on her older son's pallet, listening to the steady breathing of her two most precious treasures, she thought about her life in Palenque and was grateful for the many blessings her journey had brought. She looked forward to planning for her uncle and aunt's upcoming visit. Chanil was anxious to see them, because Tikal's royal couple had been unable to attend Sak Ayi'in's recent burial rites.

Chanil was feeling homesick and needed to reminisce with family. The next day, she would begin the plans for preparing their rooms, the banquets, and the entertainment during the important visitors' stay. Her story to Chan Kayum reminded her to tell the servants they must line the walls of the sleeping quarters with *sab'ak,* the soot to keep out the ants once again invading the palace.

Chanil smiled and remembered how one *uinal* past, the boys' little dog, Witik, yelped after being stung on the nose by a *chapat*. His curiosity had gotten the better of him as he chased and barked at the long, multi-legged insect heading toward the two playing brothers. His yelp of pain had warned the boys of the approaching pest.

"Mama, Mama!" they called out to her that day. She and Chukah ran to where the boys were playing, and as she picked up the whimpering Witik, Chukah squashed the scurrying insect in his palm. Chanil attempted to soothe the puppy's wound with a poultice of epazote leaves, but the little dog squirmed from her attentions and ran to Chukah.

"Once again, you have rescued us, Chukah. And it seems Witik is a hero, too!" she proclaimed. "Let us find your father and tell him how that little dog has saved you boys. I will tell him he must now cease his joking that if the cacao trees ever stopped growing, the priests would have to sacrifice little brown- and white-spotted Witik—the coloring most favored for sacrifice to Ek Chuah. I love the little *tz'i*. If the priests need a sacrificial animal, a blue iguana will have to substitute!"

CHAPTER THIRTY-FIVE

Later that *uinal,* the council between the region's two most important kings was soon to convene. As Queen Chanil sat at her loom, finishing a shawl she was weaving for her visiting aunt, the observant Itz'At told her all about the city's excitement so evident all around him.

"Since the council hasn't met in Palenque in many *tuns,* Palenque's residents are looking forward to seeing the great King K'awiil—not to mention Tikal's queen and their priests and slaves. There hasn't been this much excitement since your marriage, My Queen."

"Yes, Itz'At, I'm sure it is thrilling for the people to see the bright costumes of the foreigners and to hear stories of other cities. I am told the visitors are buying souvenirs of our pottery, woven goods of bright cottons, and intricate basketry as soon as they are made."

"And our food vendors can hardly keep up with the demand for Palenque's fruits and spicy meat-filled tacos," added Itz'At. "Have you had a chance to speak with your uncle and aunt yet?"

"The servants tell me that getting the visitors settled has taken all afternoon. I will speak with them tonight before the banquet. I have finished weaving this shawl, so I must leave you and make sure my preparations are going smoothly."

Before the first night's elaborate dinner began, Queen Chanil greeted her uncle and aunt in their guest room. "I am overjoyed to see you, Uncle Hasau and Aunt Twelve Macaw! I am most happy to welcome you to my home, the beautiful palace of Palenque. If you want for anything while you are here, you need only ask," Chanil said with a bow. "I trust your rooms are comfortable, and you are familiar with the latrines, steam baths, Queen's Bath, and servants' quarters. Please know if you want for anything, it is yours."

"You have made us very proud, Chanil." King K'awiil smiled and lovingly took his niece's hand. "Your life has changed so much during your reign here. We cannot know why our beloved Sak Ayi'in was taken from us, but we are here for you now."

Just then, their servants alerted them that the festivities and banquet were about to begin. "I look forward to hearing more about your life here, my dear." Her aunt embraced her, and they all headed for the banquet hall.

As the dinner guests feasted, dancers and musicians entertained the large audience. Chanil clapped her hands and smiled when she saw a dancer wearing a costume with huge wings made of bird feathers. The crowd applauded when another one danced with a giant albino boa. All the guests were fascinated by the entertainment and enjoyed the food. The dancing and music were as beautiful as Chanil had hoped and continued until every last sweetened corn cake was served.

After dinner, Tikal's king addressed his niece once again. "You have become an exceptional queen and an even more beautiful mother. My brother, Ah Mac, would have been so proud of you."

"Thank you, Uncle Hasau." Chanil bowed and gestured to K'in Balam and to her nursemaid, who held little Chan Kayum. As they approached, Chanil continued, "I am most proud of my sons. K'in Balam has performed his designation rights, and Chan Kayum is learning to play flute music. My guard, Chukah Nuk T'zi, is a formidable teacher of the clay flute. Have you met him yet?"

"Chanil, I couldn't help but notice him!" her uncle declared. "I have seen many special courtiers in all sizes and shapes, but this one is the largest man I have ever witnessed. If he weren't protecting you and the children, Chanil, I would pay a high price for him at *my* court.

"Now, K'in Balam." King K'awiil bent to address his nephew. "Perhaps you could take me on a tour of your part of the palace and tell me what you, as First Sprout, have been learning in your studies to be the greatest king of Palenque!"

K'in Balam scampered to King K'awiil's side and straightened as tall as he could to appear as kingly as possible to his famous great-uncle. "With your permission, Mama." The boy bowed low to his mother and took the visiting king's hand. "I would like to show our quarters to your uncle. I would also like to take him to the ball court to show him how three temples look down on our court. Surely ours would rival Tikal's in artwork and size!"

Chanil and her uncle smiled at each other. K'in Balam couldn't know that Tikal boasted a triple ball court revered in all of the Maya lands.

"We go, then!" King K'awiil proclaimed, and they marched out of the banquet room as proud as two kings.

The next day, Akal and King Hasau Chan K'awiil II rode on litters carried atop four sturdy slaves each for a tour of Akal's burial site. Lord Akal was glad for the opportunity to speak to his ally of his concerns regarding the problems of morale in Palenque.

Both men left their litters and climbed the stairway to the construction site. King Akal gestured to the temple being built over a demolished building within sight of the palace. He could see Cab Men Tun meticulously counting out lengths with his measuring cord as he explained the dimensions for a wall to a foreman. Akal was proud of this monument dedicated to his greatness as king.

"It has been determined the *k'ulel* energy is most intense here at this old temple site; therefore, I have chosen this place for my burial. The construction will probably take five *tuns* to complete. I only hope we will not need the temple workers for war in the meantime.

"Many Maya cities have fallen, Hasau. Yaxchilán was like a restless and temperamental child who coveted every tribute to me. They conquered and ruled Piedras Negras, and then their people overran the monarchy. Now there is nothing left of either city. I hear stories like this daily. It seems conflict never stops."

"I know that Calakmul has barely a city left, but they may also want to weaken Palenque's strength, Akal." King K'awiil lowered his voice. "I don't think the prying ears of the servants tending the litters can hear us, but the less they know of the problems in the Maya lands, the better.

"The other cities such as Toniná and Sak T'zi still show strength, but they all want what they can't produce—Palenque's cacao, *k'uk* feathers, corn, and workers as well. We have also heard the grumbling of unhappiness among my people in Tikal. Can you blame them?"

Akal nodded in agreement. "The peasants are hungry and fearful they will be sacrificed to the gods for rain and more abundant crops. Medicines are harder to come by with the clearing of the rain forest around our cities. We are in constant need of sufficient wood for building and for fires to burn the limestone."

"Sometimes I think we are destroying the mother who feeds us, Akal," continued King K'awiil. "You have a river nearby, but in Tikal, we rely on rain for our crops. I worry each year those rains won't come. Our plastered cisterns will dry out after two *tuns* without rain. And as you know, we cannot store our corn for more than two *tuns,* or it will rot."

"Here in Palenque," added King Akal, "it is already increasingly difficult for our farmers to feed their own families, much less the growing elite class. It seems fewer babies are surviving in these times. What about stories of fear and rebellion that are spread by the *Puuc* traders?"

King K'awiil watched the backbreaking labor going on in the huge pit below. Workers were constructing the stone stairway that would lead down to Akal's crypt and the serpent-like airway duct alongside it that stretched from the burial chamber to the unfinished temple above. "I have noticed escalating trade brings gossip and fear from one city to the next, because each wants what the next has. Yet we kings must keep up a strong front and make our cities and monuments bigger and better than those of our neighbors. Perhaps these actions destroy our people, from whom we gain our strength."

Both kings grew quiet as they looked out at Akal's final resting place.

"Let us discuss these concerns at our last council assembly tomorrow. If we don't stop this undercurrent of unrest, the last of the great Maya cities will be at risk." King Akal strode back to the waiting litters. "Come, Hasau, let us smoke together and plan our final meeting. It may be the most important discussion we will have of this *Yahau!*"

CHAPTER THIRTY-SIX

Akal sat on his throne in the holy *Zac Nuk Na* temple. Accompanying him were King K'awiil and their cities' most important *sahals*—and as always, Keh Cahal and Ah Kan Mai were in attendance. They passed the ceremonial cigar around and spoke comfortably in the presence of Itz'At and the fan bearers.

"I want no more problems with Toniná and Tortaguero," Akal began. "We are here to speak about solutions—and ways we can appease the people who work hard for our cities."

"They are hungry, Your Majesty," offered the *sahal*, Tilot. "The people want to work, but they also want to feed their children. They hear of sackings of great cities by invaders, aided by the peasants. I hope *my* workers are not planning similar actions."

"Tilot, you own land and have a large family to feed. I know you speak with other heads of elite clans. Has anyone offered you solutions?" asked Akal.

"Yes, those land owners want to subjugate the workers even more. Gossipers and foreigners bring tales of how other great Maya cities have fallen. The family heads are beginning to let fear dictate their interactions with the workers.

"My neighbor had to threaten his foreman with Ah Kan Mai's knife on the *chac mool* stone. The man only became belligerent with the threats. My neighbor needed this foreman's help with the other workers, so he neglected to punish the man, allowing him to go back to work. I believe this weakness on my neighbor's part has only made the situation worse."

"I am hearing similar stories in *my* city, as well," King K'awiil offered. "The people are beginning to gain an upper hand. This is dangerous. Only the promise of conquest in battle and treasures from other cities can appease them. We must continue to instill fear in the people. That is our only strength! I will go home and build my army even bigger, and I suggest you do the same, Akal. Our people are like children and can be distracted for the time being."

"Perhaps you are right, Hasau," Akal said. "There seems to be no choice but to war with our neighbors once more."

The men all began talking at once, each one shouting above the other with solutions and suggestions. The only thing that got them quiet was the appearance of great platters of food being brought into the room.

"Hasau, it is easy to temporarily forget a king's problems when the aroma of turkey in various sauces and jugs of free-flowing *balché* all promise immediate satisfaction," Akal said to his ally as they sat to eat.

"Akal, my niece, Chanil, has appeared to step into the role of queen with little difficulty. You can thank my brother, Men Lamat, for that," King K'awiil said as he ate. "When she left Tikal with him and their retinue, I must admit, I worried about what her life would be like here."

"Keh Cahal led the entire group to the safety of Palenque. I trust him to watch my back in war, as well." Akal lifted his cup to his top soldier, who sat next to him.

"It was my duty and my honor, Great *Ahau*. And King K'awiil … you can be very proud of your niece. She has proved to be the purpose this city needed."

"Queen Chanil is like a precious jewel to me. I often wonder why the gods have blessed me with such a gift," King Akal said to the men, feeling relaxed with the food and *balché*. As he turned to Keh Cahal, his face became serious. "I hope it never comes to it, but if I die on the battlefield, I hope you will protect her and my sons until the boys are old enough to rule. I know her uncle would want her back in Tikal, but her duties are now here."

"I am aware of her place in Palenque, My King. You know I will do whatever you wish. Your family is very important to me … to all of us." Keh Cahal appeared uncomfortable as he rose and bowed to both kings. "It is time I leave you two monarchs to your discussions."

"I hope the food hasn't upset him," King Akal said, watching the soldier head for the doorway.

"He may find our family conversation boring, Akal. As long as he remains the fine soldier he is, that is what is important. This meeting has proven to be very important, Akal. I think we have settled some major concerns."

King K'awiil was anxious to speak to Men Lamat after the long morning meeting and the scheduled ball game. It was now mid-afternoon before Tikal's king could finally visit his brother. King K'awiil felt uncomfortable seeing his sibling looking so old and frail. His own portly frame was in sharp contrast to the older man's delicate body. He had chosen to visit his brother while Men Lamat had his midday meal in the old priest's chambers. With a flourish, two servants set out hot rolled tortillas stuffed with black beans and chilies accompanied by a tasty stew of deer meat and fresh vegetables. King K'awiil eyed the meal and gave in to eating once more with gusto while Men Lamat merely picked at his food.

"I believe the food here in Palenque quite outshines ours in Tikal. I hope Lady Twelve Macaw has had our servants procure some of these recipes from the cook!

"How has your life been here in Palenque, Men Lamat? Has teaching Chanil's young sons worn you out?" King K'awiil's attempts at humor with his brother only brought a smile to the old man's lips.

"Raising Chanil and helping her to prepare her sons for kingship has been my life's work. I shall go to *Xibalbá* a contented man, my brother."

"Let us not talk prematurely of the afterlife, Men Lamat, unless you are suffering from a disease you aren't telling me about. With the kind of food they serve here, you should be as big as I am. Yet you have lost much weight. What have your visions told you?"

"My visions are getting cloudy, my brother. Yes, although the food is delicious, I have a pain in my gut that worries me. I am ready to leave this old body, but I hate to leave Chanil to that snake, Ah Kan Mai."

"Surely she is protected by the giant and her husband. Anyone would be a fool to try to harm her," King K'awiil said, trying to assure *himself* more than his older brother.

"Brute strength is no match for the high priest's magic." Men Lamat pushed away his unfinished meal. "I am now at that place where I must let go and accept the fate of the gods. Chanil is protected by them, and I find comfort in that."

"If you think it is warranted, I can speak with Akal about Ah Kan Mai," offered the king. "Chanil is a treasure to him and has brought him the heirs he has prayed for."

"Akal trusts the high priest. Ultimately, we must place our fate in the gods, Hasau," was Men Lamat's weary response.

King K'awiil could see his brother was tired and needed sleep. He left the room and pondered the wisdom of marrying off his beautiful niece to a king with a treacherous household. He couldn't convince her to come back to Tikal for a lengthy visit now. She had the young child to care for, and her oldest son was deep in his studies. He realized he had to trust what the gods planned for her.

CHAPTER THIRTY-SEVEN

Lady Twelve Macaw sat on her bed, admiring the many gifts presented to her on the visit to Palenque. Soon her niece would be there to finally have a quiet talk uninterrupted by official meetings. It would be their last time together before she and Tikal's king left for home in the morning.

Chanil bowed low as she entered her aunt's room. Lady Twelve Macaw was suddenly aware of how old and changed she must appear to Chanil. Tikal's queen wore a brightly woven jacket and stiff collar topped by heavy jewelry that added to her considerable size—befitting a wealthy queen.

"Come in, my dearest Chanil," the older queen beckoned. "I often wondered how an innocent girl was going to handle the role of queen of a foreign land, but I see I needn't have worried. You have blossomed into a beautiful woman and mother. It can't be easy being Second Wife to a powerful king. Tell me, is it hard to cope with the First Wife's family?"

Finding no room on the bed to sit near her aunt, Chanil curled up at her feet like the young girl in Tikal of so many years past. "They ignore me most of the time, so I am not troubled by Lady Zac Ku or her daughter, Lady Yax Koh. Even though we live very near one another, I don't see them much.

"Sometimes I feel lonely, especially now, without Sak Ayi'in ... but my duties and my children keep me busy here. And I am so happy you have come!" She smiled her exquisite smile that brought Lady Twelve Macaw's attention from the trinkets back to her niece once again.

"I don't know who else to talk to, dear Aunt, but I feel I am in danger. I sought out the *chilan* who predicted my sons' births, but I am told she took too much of the toad's venom and died. I would have liked to know her predictions."

"That is very unfortunate. I rely on my fortune-teller as a sure source of information. Could you be in danger from Lady Zac Ku and her daughter? I hear the younger woman is too old now to give Akal a grandson, and I know how palace politics work. I am sure she resents your being here and giving Akal two sons. Be alert to the quiet dangers women can reveal," Lady Twelve Macaw whispered.

"I don't believe they are a part of a conspiracy; I think it is really just the high priest, Ah Kan Mai, who has never wanted me here. I'm sure he is planning something—and probably for a time when Akal is away. My dreams warn me of a snake hiding and waiting to strike." Chanil's voice became soft, and she suddenly shivered. "Uncle Men Lamat is old and frail now, and Akal is often gone. Thankfully, he has appointed the giant, Chukah, to guard me. Have you seen him?"

"He would be difficult to miss, my dear." Her aunt laughed. "But are you safe alone with him?" Her eyes narrowed.

"Absolutely! He is sworn to protect my sons and me. It is so strange, Aunt—it is as though he can read my mind. I merely have to think something, and Chukah is there for my every wish. He looks rather frightful, yet he is gentle. He doesn't speak, but he hears our commands. I find him comforting to be around. My life here in Palenque may be in danger from the plans of a priest; yet I have the help of a giant, and ultimately, I am in the hands of the gods."

Lady Twelve Macaw thought with sadness how wise her niece had become in such a short time. "Growing into motherhood has brought you maturity and enhanced your beauty. In spite of the fear you are expressing, you carry yourself with grace and confidence. Don't reveal your apprehensions to any of the servants. One doesn't know to whom they gossip. Although palace life has its advantages, the disadvantages are many and may be dangerous. You can come back to Tikal anytime you wish, Chanil. I miss having you and your sister with me."

"Thank you, dear Aunt, but my duties here are many—most importantly, those to my husband and children. I must leave you now, but if I may help you prepare for your trip home, please call me. My servant, Muluc, would be happy to help as well."

The older woman watched Chanil bow and leave the room with her head held high. Tikal's queen was sorry they were to leave in the morning. Lady Twelve Macaw closed her eyes and silently offered a special prayer for her niece's wisdom and strength in the days ahead. She and King K'awiil would be back in Tikal, Akal would wage another campaign, and Chanil would be left alone in Palenque with the devious Ah Kan Mai. The young queen would need the help of the gods—since the priest had the powers of magic at his disposal.

CHAPTER THIRTY-EIGHT

M en Lamat lay in his bed, glad the palace had returned to normal now that the visitors had left. He had no energy to observe K'in Balam's studies with Itz'At or to sit in the garden with his beloved niece and watch her play with Chan Kayum. The old teacher still didn't feel as though his journey to Xibalbá was imminent. Nonetheless, his unease made him reach for the four dried peyote buttons at his bedside. That pretty servant girl, Mu'ut Ek, had brought them while she thought he was sleeping. Watching her leave, he chuckled to himself that he was still not too old to appreciate her young breasts barely visible under her thin *po't.*

Over the years, Men Lamat had used the dried cactus tops for divining purposes. He reached for them even more lately to ease the pain in his joints—and the more worrisome pain in his gut. Sometimes he smoked them ground and sprinkled over his tobacco, or lately, he just chewed two or three to feel pain-free and venture to the magic realm of his visions.

Since his appetite had been diminishing lately, Men Lamat knew they would have an even greater effect that night. He was a little hungry, since that young servant had taken away his uneaten lunch when she left. *No matter,* the old man thought. *After I rest and seek a vision, I will call for more food. Perhaps she'll return with my dinner and sit with me a while.*

Men Lamat put all four of the cactus buttons in his mouth and began to chew. *These taste strange,* he thought. Bitterness clawed at the back of his tongue, yet he was perplexed by a honey-like sweetness that clung to the insides of his cheeks. In a moment, the room began to spin.

What is that huge shape coming in the door? Men Lamat found himself unable to speak, but his mind screamed out the question, *Who are you?* Then, in the dim light of his wall torch, he saw a *cib* the size of a man fly to the ceiling and then drop heavily on top of him, crushing his chest. The huge bird ripped open Men Lamat's belly and began to feast on his intestines. *But I am not dead! You vultures do not feast on the living … stop! Oh, Great Yum Chom, please stop your servant from eating me alive!*

It was Itz'At who found the old priest dead that night, his eyes and mouth frozen open in horror.

Poor old Men Lamat; his heart has stopped in his old age, the scribe thought as he reached for a blanket to cover the awful sight from the curious servants clustering outside the old man's room.

"Go back to your duties! No one is to enter here while I go for the queen!" the small man commanded with authority. He headed for the queen's rooms.

"What happened, Itz'At?" commanded King Akal, who held tight to his weeping wife.

"I took Men Lamat his dinner and found him dead, Your Majesty. My Queen, I am so sorry you have lost your beloved uncle." He bowed, aware of her anguish.

King Akal spoke for his grief-stricken wife. "Thank you, Itz'At. We will call for Men Lamat's assistants to take care of his body. Tomorrow, we shall have a ceremony of mourning. Let us hope my wife will not have to endure any more sorrow after this!" the king declared, gesturing to his servants to gather the other priests.

"Your uncle will certainly be missed, Chanil. I will make sure he is well taken care of," was all Akal could manage to say. He left Chanil to her servant girl and walked with Itz'At to the corridor outside of Men Lamat's room.

"First her sister, now her uncle. I am at a loss to help my beloved Chanil. I liked Men Lamat very much and appreciated how the old priest helped turn my wife into a true queen. I am grateful he patiently taught K'in Balam so much about Palenque's past, and how to represent our family as a royal prince. The queen has had a heavy load to carry. I only wanted my beautiful wife to be happy, but there are some things even I can't control!"

Chanil was finally left alone to mourn. She sat in a chair near her uncle and felt some peace just being in the same room with him. When her father died, and later her mother, it was Uncle Men Lamat who comforted her. Recently, when her sister died, she buried her grief on his old, kind shoulders. Now he was gone, and she felt more alone than at any other time in her life.

It was Men Lamat who had prepared her as a young girl for her *Mik' chal 'uh*—her rites of adulthood—and coached her how to pierce her tongue to achieve the most blood with the least amount of damage. The life of a young girl whose exceptional beauty would rouse jealousy and suspicion was difficult without parents. With his caring ways and genuine love for her, he taught her which herbs to use for all ailments, including *chaya* tea for monthly pains. He showed her where to find the sacred mushrooms and how to squeeze the giant frog's neck gland for ritual potions. He taught her how men think and how they react. He prepared her for life as queen, and she would have to continue on with only his memory.

With each loss, I have found my own strength. I pray the gods will show me how to be strong for my sons now.

"How unfortunate—yet another death in the woman of Tikal's family," Ah Kan Mai declared from his tower room. "Well, don't just stand there." He gestured impatiently to his assistant. "Go assist with his burial preparations." As soon as the high priest was alone, he allowed himself a broad smile. His new little servant girl, Mu'ut Ek, had performed perfectly. As directed, the comely girl reported to him as soon as she had taken old Men Lamat the medicinal cactus buttons Ah Kan Mai had prepared.

How sad she will have to mysteriously leave the palace when I don't need her anymore; the girl is such a pleasure to look at. The gods sent her to me, and they will help me do away with her when the time comes. Now the young queen is my last challenge.

Ah Kan Mai had been carefully collecting Palenque's greatest codices and storing them in his tower. After all, he held the important position of *ah k'u hun*—Keeper of the Royal Archives. It wasn't hard to explain to the curious under-priests how the valuable histories would be safe in his possession from rain, flooding, or thieves.

But his plan didn't end there. The high priest had already begun hiring porters to transport these holy manuscripts of Palenque's history and knowledge—a few at a time—to the perfect cave he had discovered years ago, high in the mountains. There, Palenque's most precious of treasures would be safe. The porters knew their destination, but Ah Kan Mai had also hired *Puuc* traders to lie in wait for the returning porters and swiftly eliminate them. This way, no one but *he* knew the exact location of the caves. In just a few more trips, the priest would be ready to use this perfect cache against anyone who got in the way of his ruling Palenque when the king was gone.

Since the arrival of that woman from Tikal, King Akal had become a besotted idiot who cared more for his sons and wife than for Palenque. It looked like one more campaign was coming soon, and he strongly encouraged the king to go to war once again. It was imperative the king be away from the city for the priest's plans to take shape. His visions told him a big event was to occur in the near future, but the exact nature of the occurrence was still murky. Ah Kan Mai needed to delve into his magic more, but for the present, he would make himself ready to assume more power when the king was away.

He was also aware the giant was becoming too attached to the children and the young queen. The priest needed the huge dog to do his bidding, as was originally intended. He chuckled as he imagined how well his big, mute *tz'i* would perform. Yes, it was almost time.

CHAPTER THIRTY-NINE

King Akal Balam felt more tired than usual; his arms and legs were weary from the previous day's battle. After one *uinal* of fighting, he hoped today would be the deciding conflict. His men were camped just outside of Sak Tz'i; the initial raids against the city had proven successful. They had destroyed all new buildings and had taken several prisoners. Sak T'zi's water supply was plentiful, and the food was, too. But the city's people were far more resilient than Akal had expected. As the king drank his morning *posol* in the quiet and coolness of the dawn, he thought of Chanil and his sons at home in Palenque and how they waited for his return, not knowing the horror Akal faced with each day's battle. This campaign had begun with the same fervor his young warriors usually showed, but he had noticed the beginnings of doubt as they valiantly fought over the past three very hot and humid days.

His old servant helped him get into his battle clothes. "Chan Och, I appreciate your looking after my sore old joints when our skirmishes are done for the day. I'm sure it hasn't escaped you how long it now takes to soothe my muscles at night and to get me ready for battle the next morning."

"We both are no longer young, My King. Is it possible for you to rest today and let Keh Cahal lead the men alone? He is a fine war chief, and your men know what to do." The old servant slipped the quilted armor on Akal's outstretched arms.

"Sak T'zi is a small but renegade province, Chan Och. To prevent any doubt about our victory, my men need to see their king out there with them. Now, go ask Keh Cahal to come join me in one last cup of *posol* before we begin today's warfare."

"Are you ready for this day's fight, Akal?" Keh Cahal bowed and crossed his clenched fist across his chest.

"I hope today ends our conflict. We're all fatigued. Too many of your elite guard are wounded, and after one *uinal* of battle, I'm beginning to worry, Keh Cahal."

"Then let us now give our men a rousing speech and a promise of victory, Akal. I have been surprised at the strength of Sak T'zi's young soldiers, but no army is better than ours. Come, let us show them who rules the region!"

The clash began just as the sun broke through the mists. In the jumble of feathered headdresses and brightly colored costumes, Palenque's warriors charged forward into the fray. First, the black painted *holcans* cleared the way for the spear-throwers and hatchet soldiers, and waiting to strike were Keh Cahal's elite guard. With renewed vigor, Sak T'zi's soldiers faced them head on, spears aloft and screaming prayers to their gods.

The voices of dying young soldiers crying out pierced the air over the cacophony of sounds from screaming of monkeys and birds and the thud of stone clubs hitting skulls. The *tax* war drums of both sides thrummed, and the *hom ta* trumpets encouraged all to fight for their lives. The battle continued as the sun rose high in the sky. Dead warriors from both sides lay about, and among them laid those unlucky ones who wished death would come soon. Prisoners from both sides labored at clearing the dead bodies from the field, which was red with blood.

It was hot beneath Akal's battle dress. His cumbersome headdress and heavy jaguar skin tunic were wet with sweat. His men around him fought to protect their king as he did away with the two nearest enemy attackers. Akal saw Keh Cahal behead a Sak T'zi soldier nearby and felt proud that his friend was such an excellent warrior.

Just then, pain seared Akal's right arm. *Xibalbá! A spear has just sliced my right arm!* "Take this, you pile of *ta'!*" Akal cursed his enemy attacker and himself for allowing a moment of distraction. Akal deflected the soldier's .hatchet with his own. The young man was strong, but Akal knocked him down with a deft blow from his left fist. With strength and speed, he grabbed the soldier's topknot of hair and stabbed him in the chest with his spear.

Akal stood to inspect the wound on his own arm. *It is not that deep a wound, after all,* he thought. But suddenly, he felt pain again—this time in his stomach! Doubling over, he could only gasp, *"Aaahhh!"*

"Akal? Akal!" The king looked up to see Keh Cahal's shocked expression as his war chief ran toward him. Akal slumped forward in pain, clutching the spear protruding from his gut. With his obsidian hatchet, Keh Cahal hacked the foreign attacker to death, all the while screaming obscenities at the man.

The pain was unlike anything Akal had ever felt. His blood spewed as Keh Cahal pulled the spear out and carefully removed his cotton armor. He felt himself losing awareness at times. It was hard to speak. "Keh Cahal ... I think this is the end for me. I am no good to my men now, and they shouldn't see me like this. Get me out of here ... can you take me home to Chanil before I die?"

"I vow to get you back to Palenque as soon as we can. It will take three days if we can move quickly. I will staunch the blood flow as best I can, and our *x'man* will apply whatever medicine we have on hand. Please, Akal, stay awake and fight death so that you may see the queen and your sons again."

"If I go to *Xibalbá,* Keh Cahal, please take care of the queen for me. You're the only man I trust. Do I have your promise?"

"Of course, My King. I will do whatever you ask of me."

"Thank you ... gods in the heavens, this hurts ... I have to see my family again ..."

Keh Cahal sprung into action. "I need two men to help me carry our *Ahau* to safety! The rest of you ... avenge your king!" Palenque's panicked soldiers stood there, staring in disbelief.

"Now!"

CHAPTER FORTY

AD 879

From his observatory tower, Ah Kan Mai was the first to see the brilliant ball of light as it crossed the night sky. His pulse quickened. This was the sign he had been praying for while Palenque's king and army were away at war with Sak T'zi. He alerted the priests and told them this was a sign from the gods—a portent of something ominous—perhaps the beginning of Palenque's decline. He ordered Itz'At to record this auspicious event in his current codex. The next day, the conch shell blasts would call the cowering peasants from their huts to observe Ah Kan Mai's sacrificial offering to the gods to protect their king and Palenque.

The high priest's prediction turned out to be true. Within a few days of the omen and under cover of darkness, Keh Cahal brought his wounded king home to Palenque. The soldier stood before Queen Chanil and Ah Kan Mai and spoke in whispers of King Akal, who lay barely conscious and in obvious pain on a pallet in his room.

"My Queen, the king suffered a spear to his stomach several days ago. We knew we must secretly bring him back home as fast as our soldiers could carry the litter. We hired a *Puuc* trader at the Usumacinta River to pilot the *kayuk* that would bring our great

Ahau here. He has not spoken since yesterday ... I am sorry, Your Majesty."

"You did what Akal would have expected of you, Keh Cahal," was all Queen Chanil said.

Ah Kan Mai knew it was only a matter of time before the rumors began to spread by the *Puuc* pilot to the other cities about Akal's mortal wound.

"I will be the first to administer to the king, Your Majesty," insisted Ah Kan Mai to the distraught Chanil. "My knowledge of medicine is superior, and I prefer to dress his wounds in private." The priest read Chanil's helpless expression and knew he was now in control. The salves, broths, and teas he would give King Akal were his own preparations. Ah Kan Mai's wrath would keep those lower priests quiet who might question whether the king's condition worsened under his care.

The next evening, Keh Cahal entered the king's chamber and saw Chanil sitting stoically with Akal and speaking softly to him. Observing her with the king, he knew the event she dreaded the most was here. All she could do was help care for Akal and assure her sons their father was in the hands of the gods. The soldier saw her own preparations of honey and herb-filled clay bottles placed on a table near her wounded husband's bed.

"Your Majesty, has he been able to speak to you?" She only shook her head as she sat there. "Please allow me to sit with the king tonight so you may get some rest. Your sons need you more than your husband does now."

Queen Chanil looked like a sad child. She pressed her forehead to the old, thin hand she desperately clasped in her own. "If he awakens, I want to be here," she said, looking up at the captain. Her moist eyes pierced his heart.

"I will call for you if he stirs," assured Keh Cahal.

With that encouragement, she rose and looked at her husband's most trusted soldier. As their eyes met, the soldier wondered if she also felt a surge of strength and hope rush through her body, as he did. He extended a hand to her and she fell forward into his arms. He wanted Chanil to feel safe for a moment—just as she had so long ago in Chinkultic, as though the world could not touch her here. But the world intruded, and she pulled away.

"Thank you," the young queen murmured, not meeting his eyes.

"Please know I am here for you, My Lady." Keh Cahal wanted to hold her again. "You will have many decisions to make. As I am Akal's right hand, I pray I will also have *your* trust."

"We must speak soon," was all Chanil could manage to say. She walked out the king's doorway.

The next day, Keh Cahal called for a meeting in the war room with Chanil and two of his most trusted soldiers.

Keh Cahal spoke gently but firmly. "Your Majesty, Akal's condition is not improving in spite of the best medicines we have. This is the reason I have asked you to come here. Although the life of constant labor seems to move along normally for the peasants, the palace is in a somber and confused state. It is important you are informed of palace protocol in this sad but not unusual situation. K'in Balam is too young to assume the duties of king, but you, as his mother, must rule as regent until he comes of age—just as the great Pakal's mother did until he assumed the throne at the age of twelve *tuns*."

"I feel so helpless and unprepared for the future, Keh Cahal," the young queen said. "What of the First Wife or her daughter? Might they assume control of Palenque?"

"Without an heir from Lady Zac Ku's daughter, the obvious choice to rule is you, as the mother of Akal's sons. There might be the annoying existence of Lady Zac Ku's power-hungry brother, but I plan to have a direct and unflinching talk with him to dispel any aspirations he might have.

"Please know you are not alone at this time. I am here to offer you strength and advice. Palenque's army is behind you, and so is the faith and love of the people."

Over the next five days, the king's health appeared to rally. Ah Kan Mai held a special ceremony in which all of the royals pierced their earlobes and tongues and sent their blood burning up to the heavens in a plea for their king. After the ceremony, he addressed the old queen in her rooms.

"Lady Zac Ku, it is evident you stay here in your part of the palace most of the time. I strongly suggest you go to your husband more often. It is important that you are seen visiting with the king," Ah Kan Mai advised. "The servants spread gossip, and before long, even the field workers know our business."

"It is as if my life is ending along with my spouse. I know Akal's death is near, and so is my realization that Palenque will now succumb to the leadership of the Second Wife and her sons. As you suggest, I will continue to make brief late afternoon visits to the king's beside, and other than at those times, no one shall see me."

"Do not release your influence as First Wife to that intruder from Tikal just yet, My Queen. You are still the First Wife of Palenque's king, and the people love you. I predict you may still regain your position."

"I have no power without Akal," she muttered as she limped off.

Ah Kan Mai knew it was time to finally put his plans in place. He called for an urgent meeting with Palenque's priests.

With difficulty, he masked the excitement in his voice. "I needn't remind you of the king's imminent death. It will be up to us to keep the leadership of Palenque running smoothly, and I now have authority from Lady Zac Ku to proceed where she is unable. It is clear that control of Palenque should be in our hands, due to our knowledge of all things. Those who ally themselves with me will be assured of high positions under my new regime. The king's sons will then be groomed to rule Palenque over the many years between now and their maturity. The king and I have spoken many times on this subject, and these are his direct wishes, as well."

"What about Queen Chanil? Won't she rule as regent?" an older priest asked.

"Perhaps very soon, she can be persuaded to return to Tikal, her *real* home." The piercing look from Ah Kan Mai ended further discussion. He left them whispering to one another about his directive and headed for his next important meeting.

❧

A soft tinkling of shells warned Chukah the high priest was approaching the queen's rooms.

"Chukah Nuk T'zi! You will come to my observatory tomorrow at the midday meal, when the queen is with the king. She won't need you lurking outside her door at that time, and the boys will be with their tutors. I know I do not have to remind you how I saved you from death many *tuns* ago, and it was I who procured this easy and clean work for you here in the palace."

Chukah bowed in assent. It was true; his queen was so preoccupied with the ailing king that she was only in her rooms at night, and the nurses and palace residents kept the boys busy. It was good that Chukah never spoke; he allowed other people to do all the talking. The priest would reveal his intentions.

"I have important plans for you, so don't be late."

He watched Ah Kan Mai leave. *The spider is about to attack.*

CHAPTER FORTY-ONE

"Well, Chukah. Although you appear slow and simple, you do take instruction very well." The high priest addressed the giant man who now stood at his tower room doorway. "I have ordered a servant girl to bring us a delicious meal, and then I'll begin to instruct you as to how you may repay me for all these years of palace life, you fortunate dog!" Ah Kan Mai could hardly control his happiness. At last, his plans would now come to fruition.

"Mu'ut Ek, you may set the food down here next to my very large friend." Both men watched the attractive servant girl position the tray on a table between them. "She is quite a ripe and juicy plum, isn't she, Chukah? Perhaps if you obey my requests, you will be able to taste her sweetness!" Ah Kan Mai laughed as the frightened girl hurried out of the room.

"What was I saying?" Ah Kan Mai watched the giant's eyes follow Mu'ut Ek's exit. "Oh, yes ... your debt to me. You may begin eating, but try not to think about comely Mu'ut Ek as you bite into one of those plums." He laughed again and gestured to the food-laden table. Chukah's huge hand trembled slightly as the giant slave reached for the ripe fruit.

"And here, drink some of this *balché* I had prepared earlier. I know you never get ripe plums or *balché*—isn't that true?" Ah Kan Mai watched the huge servant gulp down the fermented bark drink he had personally laced with his own blend of sweet-tasting herbs, a preparation to numb the giant's mind and open it to suggestion.

"We know no woman would be willing give herself to a man as large as you, Chukah, and certainly wouldn't want to die in childbirth with your offspring, as your own mother did. Perhaps Mu'ut Ek can be convinced to share some *balché* with you and will forget about how cumbersome you are." The priest could see that Chukah was beginning to relax with the strong and potent drink.

"I am sure you understand your life will change with the death of the king," Ah Kan Mai continued. "The queen will no longer be living here in the palace, so you may either be put to death or be allowed to accompany her to Tikal. During King K'awiil's recent visit, I overheard him expressing his desire to have you in his palace. Since Queen Chanil must be convinced to leave *without* her sons, it is possible she will only leave if a trusted servant accompanies her—someone she cares about. She must be very lonely by now for ripe fruit herself, wouldn't you imagine?" Ah Kan Mai dared to refer to the queen's celibate life of late just to see the giant's reaction. But observing Chukah's muddled expression and messy hands as he ate, the priest smiled and continued.

"I remind you once again that you would be dead if I hadn't rescued you—an insignificant worker in the quarries. Now you may learn from me how our great city of Palenque will thrive in the future." Reaching for a plum himself, he continued, "It has been decided I will reign as king, as the queen's sons are not of age as yet. There is simply no one else capable, since I have taken it upon myself to have Palenque's holy archives hidden in the mountains not far from here. When the time is right, they will be rescued from their secret place in caves unknown to anyone but me—for you see, all those idiots who did the work of hiding them are no longer in this world.

"So remember, Chukah, I still can end your life at a moment's notice. Now, as you finish your food and drink, I will describe exactly how you can help the queen, the king, and Palenque at her darkest hour."

I will convince this huge dog that he must rape the queen—a necessary act. A council of priests would surely call for her death after I say I discovered her adulterous behavior. Chukah will be forced to kidnap her, thereby "saving" her from the fate of an adulteress. She will know Palenque will need her son as king, yet she will also realize she cannot stay in the palace with her children. Only Chukah can save her and escape with her to Tikal, since the king will be dead by then. My patience will now finally be rewarded!

For the next few days, the meetings between Chukah and the priest continued at mealtimes. Ah Kan Mai heard the palace servants whispering about how they thought Chukah appeared distracted. They described how his eyes had taken on a strange stare, perhaps in grief at the ailing king's condition.

Good! Well-prepared plans fall into place quite easily.

CHAPTER FORTY-TWO

T he quiet nature and almost invisible demeanor of Palenque's chief
    scribe, Itz'At, allowed him to observe the sad and strange palace
life around him. He had heard the servants talking about meetings
of the palace workers and artisans taking place in secret. *Puuc* traders
brought tales to Palenque's merchants of well-known cities falling to
peasant unrest. Caracol and Yaxchilán were almost devoid of their
monarchy, and thousands of families were leaving for the mountains to
escape angry mobs of hungry people.

It was said that the building of monuments had stopped in nearby
Chinikhá. Palace servants also spoke about how some of the governors
of other great cities were in league with outsiders like the Mexicans
and Toltecs. These foreigners agreed to stop the mass killings and
destruction of temples in exchange for the absolute acquiescence of the
Maya nobility. Could it happen here in Palenque?

There was talk of other clandestine meetings being held in the
privacy of peasant huts. He heard the palace servants whispering about
the fate of their city when the king died. Itz'At couldn't blame them.
They were weary, and they no longer wanted to work until their bones
ached for the demanding Ah Kan Mai and the under-priests. The
people were hungry and wanted what the elite families had—real meat
to feed their families, cacao-seasoned food, and to drink cups of *balché*
sometimes. He couldn't blame them for wanting a change so the gods
would also favor *them* too, not just the elite classes.

The people had heard the stories of other cities being taken over by the peasants. They listened in awe about how the citizens of neighboring cities found the storehouses of hoarded food and grain—how they sacked the palaces and were able to feed their hungry and sick children. The unrest was quiet but growing. Itz'At feared for the queen and her sons. Perhaps he would speak to her of his concerns when she was not at the dying king's side.

Keh Cahal was distraught over the impending death of the king who was his idol and closest friend. He thought of the many years over which they had shared confidences, meals, countless cups of *balché,* and the special friendship of two men who liked and trusted one another. They had fought together many times and saved one another's lives more than once. The soldier needed to see his king one last time before his death.

The smell of rotting flesh grew stronger as Keh Cahal approached Akal's room. He stopped short as he saw Queen Chanil just outside the doorway, crying softly. Unaware of the soldier, she dried her eyes, straightened her posture, and turned to walk down the outside corridor in the direction of her sons' rooms.

"My Lady," Keh Cahal called out softly. Her face brightened when she saw him. "I want to reassure you, when the time comes … I am here for you. We must talk soon …"

"Keh Cahal, please come to my rooms after your visit with Akal. We can speak there." She turned and walked away down the colonnade. The violence of war never made Keh Cahal tremble. But each time he found himself near Queen Chanil, his heartbeat quickened, and his muscles shook. He took a deep breath and entered the king's dark chambers.

Keh Cahal knew he would always remember Akal at his best moments—in battle, encouraging his troops, or addressing the populace from atop a temple—not as a withered, chalky-skinned, helpless old man.

"Akal, I do not know if you can hear me, but I wanted to tell you goodbye, my friend. Thank you for trusting me as your right-hand man in battle and taking me into your confidence. It has been an honor to serve you. Please know I will take care of your family as though they were my own. K'in Balam will be a great king, and although Chan K'ayum is young, I will always remind him of the great man and king his father was.

"As for Queen Chanil … I pledge my life to protecting her. She has been a beautiful queen and exemplary mother. I … Akal, I …" The strong soldier lowered his head as a young son would in confessing a misdeed to his father. He couldn't tell the king he had fallen in love with the queen.

Crossing his right arm over his chest with a clenched fist in a last salute to his friend, Keh Cahal bowed and whispered, "Goodbye, My King." With that, he spun on his heels and left the room.

Keh Cahal knew palace etiquette frowned on anyone other than family in the interior of the palace after dark, but his queen had asked to speak to him in private. His last visit with the king left him feeling disheveled and lost. As he approached her door, Chanil was waiting for him. Neither noticed Chukah was not standing guard at her suite. At that moment, it would not have mattered. When Keh Cahal entered her room, neither spoke but walked into each other's arms. As they became aware of their bodies pressing desperately together, and the exciting newness of feeling each other's trembling thighs and pounding heartbeats, it was impossible for them to let go.

"Chanil, please forgive me, but I can no longer hold back my love for you," Keh Cahal whispered. "I will leave if you so wish." Finally, he released her.

"Keh Cahal, please stay with me … always," she pleaded.

With this desperate utterance, Keh Cahal held her again with more urgency, his mouth to her lips. Tasting her was more wonderful than he had imagined. She pressed against him as though she wanted to lose herself into him for a few precious moments. When Keh Cahal finally looked into her eyes, he saw what was in his heart reflected there.

"Keh Cahal, I remember my first glimpse of you many *tuns* ago as our procession entered Palenque on my marriage day. You were a strong leader of our journey. Your pride in your city was as evident as your devotion to Akal. Was it then I began to love you?"

Silently, she took his hand and led him to her bed. He watched her release her sash and lift the delicate white shift over her head. Chanil stood there, naked in the firelight that danced from the wall torches. Keh Cahal wanted to kneel at her feet, for she truly must have been descended from the gods! She had broad shoulders, perfectly shaped breasts, and a small waist. Her belly showed no stretch scars, and her hips were rounded slightly, tapering to long legs. Chanil reached for his belt and would have undressed him, but in his ardor, he quickly stepped out of his tunic and faced her.

The soldier knew he was only the second man she had ever been with, so with care and gentleness, he pulled her onto her pallet. Each kiss became more and more fervent. He allowed her to initiate what would happen next. Her sexual urgency surprised him, as did her body's natural responses to desire.

After their urgent lovemaking, the two lay there in each other's arms.

"Keh Cahal, I have never experienced painless lovemaking and absolute fulfillment. So this is what I have heard whispers about!" She laughed and buried her head in his neck. "I am sadly aware I have betrayed my husband. Perhaps he will forgive me in *Xibalbá*. But being with you has brought me unimaginable joy. How can this be so wrong, Keh Cahal?"

"Chanil, I too have experienced something with you I have never felt before. I don't want our time together to end; yet no one must know I am here. I have to leave you now, but we will be together again when it is right. I await the time when our nights can stretch lazily into mornings together." He paused to kiss her gently. "Remember, you are never alone."

Reluctantly, Keh Cahal dressed and kissed her again, uttering, "Goodbye, my only love" before he left.

CHAPTER FORTY-THREE

The king's breath was labored, and it was only a matter of time before he would be mercifully taken home to *Xibalbá* by the gods. Ah Kan Mai knew the time was right for his dim-witted slave Chukah to perform the act the priest had been pounding into his brain as he drugged and fed him over the past several days. Afterward, the giant slave could be a valuable bargaining tool to use with King K'awiil of Tikal, even though the priest never planned to actually allow the queen or her slave to reach Tikal. Things were working exactly as planned.

Chukah awoke in a stupor. The *balché* given him by the high priest had made him slump to the floor of the priest's quarters and drool down the front of his tunic as he slept. His dreams were frightening. He fought a giant *zabcán*—a rattlesnake—outside Queen Chanil's rooms in one dream. In another, strange beings appeared to him and told him he must save her from certain death in the palace. These creatures had lizard bodies and horrible eyes. They told him Queen Chanil was chosen to begin a new, pure race of Mayas. She must be taken to the holy city of Chichen Itzá, where she would be safe. *Was it a dream? It seemed so real.*

Chukah got up, and as his head began to clear, he realized he had left the queen alone while he ate and drank like a glutton. The giant stumbled back toward his station and nodded in response to Captain Keh Cahal's greeting just outside the residential rooms. *He must have been visiting the king,* thought Chukah as he fought the pain in his head and placed himself at attention at Queen Chanil's doorway. He could smell the queen's sweet scent from her room and was relieved she was safe. He sought for his clay flute in the pouch of his belt. Playing soothed his jumbled thoughts.

CHAPTER FORTY-FOUR

By afternoon of the next day, it was evident King Akal was near death. Nervous whispers ceased when Queen Chanil entered a room or when Ah Kan Mai strutted across the courtyard. It was as though the brilliance that was their king was fading—and with him, the glory that was Palenque.

With this inevitability approaching, a fearful mob of peasants left their work to gather far outside the palace grounds, beyond the elite compounds, and past the fields that struggled to nurture the people of the fading Maya jewel.

"Tonight! It must be tonight! We will do as other cities have done and take what is ours!" shouted Chukah's adoptive father, Moch Chuen. He had nothing to lose; the palace had sacrificed his daughter and taken his son. "When the royal family sleeps, we must make our move and charge the palace! There we will find enough food to feed our families. There too we will find riches to buy everything we could ever want!"

"What if the army fights us with weapons? All we have are our bare hands!" called out an older man in the crowd.

"Our whores will volunteer to keep those soldiers busy in exchange for good food tonight!" laughed another.

"We will succeed if we do this in an organized manner and tell no one other than family and close friends," Moch Chuen continued. "The element of surprise is our best weapon. We will no longer have a king by morning, so we must do this *tonight*. All in the palace must die, or we will fail at saving our families.

"Bring torches and start burning all around the palace. That will bring the sleeping nobles out of their rooms. My son, Chukah, is one of us. He will join our cause once he sees me leading our people."

"But what about the young queen and her sons?" a woman shouted above the noise.

"I said *everyone* must die! One royal person could start a monarchy all over again. Do we want to be slaves to anyone after today?" Moch Chuen eyed the crowd.

"No!" came the united response.

"We must finish burning the dry corn stalks in the fields so as not to arouse suspicion," he cautioned. "We want the corn god to bless us. Go to the fields now, as the sun sets. Sing as you work, and with all the joy in your hearts—for after this day, our world will be different. *Tonight is ours!*"

"Tonight is ours! For the people!" the peasants shouted, and they left to gather family and friends in this consummate effort.

Chanil checked on her boys, who were already asleep. She sat with them for a few moments, steeling herself for her last visit with Akal. It was peaceful in her sons' room. She smiled as she removed K'in Balam's small spear from his hand as he slept and petted little Witik's exposed muzzle as he snuggled under the covers with Chan Kayum. Their two servants were also asleep and breathing steadily. She stood and looked at her sleeping boys and hoped their dreams were happy. They couldn't know how their world was about to change.

They will become men without their father, and I will have to go on without him. It is difficult knowing I will now see Akal for the last time, but it is time to say goodbye to my husband of ten tuns.

Keh Cahal surmised that Chanil would be with her husband in his last few hours, so he went to the boys' room to sit with them until she came back to her quarters. He had to see her again. One long day had passed since their declarations of love, and he was sure she would need comforting.

The palace seemed unusually quiet. Keh Cahal's heart quickened as he saw Chanil heading toward the king's quarters. He passed the queen's doorway and walked to the boys' room. As he entered, he saw that they were sleeping; yet their servants were nowhere about. *Where are the servants? Where is Chukah, for that matter?*

Puzzled, Keh Cahal waited there to sit with the children—the offspring of the only two people he loved in the world. This was a sad time for them, and they would need to turn to a strong man. He would be there for them and their mother.

Ah Kan Mai sat at the table in his tower to enjoy a cigar laced with peyote powder. His plans were in place. The giant would have his way with the queen that night, and in the morning, the priest would say he saw the queen rutting with the slave like a she-dog in heat. Queen Chanil would be imprisoned, and his own reign would begin. The last of Palenque's codices had been taken to the mountains days ago. It was all too easy. Everything was peaceful in the palace that night. He would take charge of Palenque in the morning.

Chukah Nuk T'zi left his usual station and waited for the queen in a doorway near the king's rooms adjoining the outside colonnade that spanned the length of the royal family's quarters. A part of him thought about the gentle and loving woman she was and how defiling her body with his own huge clumsiness would make her hate him forever—just as he would hate himself. Yet this was his time to do what the gods wanted him to do. This is how he would be a part of history as well as the future. The sad, huge boy who was taunted, the giant man feared by women would be a man with a purpose!

Queen Chanil was to begin a new race of Mayas, and Chukah was the one to help the gods with her fate. He wanted to laugh at Ah Kan Mai's so-called superiority. None of the drugs the priest gave Chukah really affected the giant, except for maybe the huge quantities of *balché*. He heard everything the high priest told him. Interestingly enough, the outcome would be the same. However, he would not take the queen to Tikal, as the high priest suggested, but to the city of Chichen Itzá, the destination the ancestor's voices commanded.

He followed the queen as she left the king's chambers. He hid and watched her take a deep breath at the colonnade wall and look out at the valley. She stood there deep in thought—praying, perhaps. She began to head toward her rooms. As she neared the big boulder—the *Yax Tun*—she seemed to sense something. The queen turned in his direction, looking perplexed, but then started walking again. Suddenly, she stopped, turned abruptly, and saw him. The queen looked surprised, and he knew she felt uneasy. She addressed him.

"Chukah, I won't need you anymore tonight. You are dismissed!"

He regretted hearing the alarm in her voice; yet he could only bow in response to her command.

"I said, you are dismissed!" she repeated. He was powerless to stop what was about to happen. As he walked toward her, she stood there, eyes darting, and she appeared to consider running. The huge carved stone was between them. She stood there tall, facing him, as she had always faced uncertainty. Now he saw fear in her eyes.

She has reason to fear me. I am going to change her life forever. I pray the gods will forgive me. I pray she will forgive me.

CHAPTER FORTY-FIVE

The fall of Palenque began with the first tentative torchings just inside the walls of the palace. It spread with the rising shouts and violence. Peasants started killing dazed priests coming out of their rooms. Confusion reigned.

Keh Cahal smelled smoke and heard shouting. He ran to the hallway window and saw peasants with weapons in the patio below. With horror, he realized what was happening. He quickly awakened the boys and led them to the secret passageway near the nursery. Cautioning them to stay quiet, he carried the boys to the army training camp and shouted orders to the older men to guard them. *Where is my army?* A few very young and very old soldiers were the only ones milling about talking.

"Get your weapons, and meet me here as soon as you can!" Keh Cahal ordered the men. "The queen needs our help!" He then led the boys to the wife of a trusted old soldier. "Muwan Hun, pack some supplies, and take the princes to your home far outside the city. Keep their identity a secret, or the gods will punish you. I will retrieve them later, when it is safe."

"But Keh Cahal!" cried K'in Balam. "Let me help you defend the palace! I am a good soldier. Please let me go with you to find my mother!"

"I want my mama!" cried Chan Kayum. "And I want Witik! Where is he?"

Old Muwan Hun hugged the tired, confused boys. "Keh Cahal will find your mother. Let's go look for something to eat at my house. Perhaps Keh Cahal will bring her back there. Let him go now to defend your home."

Keh Cahal raced back to the palace with the few soldiers he could find and was appalled to see fires burning everywhere. He ran to the queen's rooms and had to step over Lady Zac Ku's lifeless body in the hallway. It was a grisly scene, with the corpses of her daughter and son-in-law near her. Alongside them was the body of a pretty servant who lay there with her clothes torn and blood pooling from between her legs. She had suffered a brutal rape as well as a hatchet to her neck.

"Chanil? Chanil!" Keh Cahal shouted frantically, but he found no evidence of her anywhere. Keh Cahal stabbed and killed three crazed peasants trying to enter the queen's bedroom. He fought the panic rising in his heart when he thought of Chanil.

Knowing his king was already gone, Keh Cahal left his soldiers to defend the palace and retreated once more through the secret escape route that brought him to the outside walls. Chanil's sons were his only concern at the present. Had their servants left them earlier to join the peasant revolt? The boys could have been killed had he not been there! He would have to get them to the safety of the mountains or die trying. The anxious soldier prayed to the gods the queen was still alive and safe someplace.

An angry group of peasants led by Moch Chuen stood at Ah Kan Mai's tower room doorway.

"Who are you people?" the priest demanded as he rose from his chair. "How dare you so rudely approach my rooms! I will have your eyes plucked out for your unruliness!" He tried to sound imperious, but a hint of fear had crept into the high priest's voice.

"We thought you would like to join your other priest friends." Moch Chuen smiled at the high priest. "Look! Down there, in the courtyard," Chukah's father ordered as he and two other peasants grabbed Ah Kan

Mai's arms. They shoved him to the window and forced him to look down at the dead bodies strewn about.

"No! Please!" Ah Kan sputtered. "You need me! Only *I* have the secrets of the priests ... of the great Maya ancestors!"

"We don't need you and your secrets, you snake! All we need is food, and we don't need *you* for that!"

"I can get you food ... anything you want! Please don't hurt me ..."

"Kill him! Kill him!" the peasants shouted, and they charged forward.

Ah Kan Mai only had time to gasp in horror before they hurled him out of his fourth-story window to the hewn rock patio below. They watched the priest's body convulse a few moments before it settled into a misshapen heap. Ah Kan Mai's broken neck twisted his head at a grotesque angle; his sightless eyes faced upward toward the tower.

"Palenque belongs to us!" cried Moch Chuen. "I'm going to look for my son. You others ... take what you want. Let us feed our people!"

EPILOGUE

The holy city of Chichen Itzá was huge, and two more inhabitants were hardly noticed—except for the giant man who found work in the limestone quarries. His traveling companion, a beautiful but silent woman, was given a home in the palace and work as a servant there. Her kitchen skills were appreciated as well as the exquisite weaving and embroidery work she did for the king and queen.

Word spread that the city of Palenque had fallen, but no one knew if any of the royalty had survived. It was assumed all were dead, including the First Wife and daughter of the great Akal Balam, his new wife and her children, and all of the priests and nobles. It was said the fire from the peasant sacking could be seen for many miles in the four directions.

I was a new servant and worked as a painter of pottery in the palace at Chichen Itzá. Women such as I were often given the job of painting court scenes on fine pottery. Because of my exceptional talent, my work was quickly accepted, and I was invited to live in the palace. Not long after my arrival, I noticed a new attendant as she sat with her loom by a window—a sad figure silently weaving a brilliant tapestry.

At first, Chanil didn't recognize me, but when I removed my turban and spoke in my own soft but male voice, she immediately recognized me as Itz'At, her court scribe in Palenque.

"Itz'At! I can't believe it is you! Please—tell no one who I am, I beg you."

"My dear Queen, I vow to keep your identity a secret, and I know you will protect mine. It is best we allow others to think we have only met here, having fled prior lives in other disrupted cities. I invite you to the tranquility of my room following tonight's evening meal. No one will disturb what appears to be two women talking after dinner."

"I look forward to learning what your experiences were before the end, Itz'At, and to share many memories with you. I have lived through so much you could not have personally witnessed. I have trusted you since we first met, and I am able to talk to you from my heart."

Later that evening, we sat in silence for a while before I spoke to the woman who sat across from me as though an equal.

"My Queen—I address you thus, because you will always be my queen—are you well? How are you coping with the loss of your sons? I grieve often that we may never know what has happened to those two fine young boys."

"I weep daily, Itz'At. When I hear the laughter of children or the haunting notes of the ceramic flute, I find it hard to continue with my duties. But I am fortunate to have clean work here in the palace, so I take my thoughts elsewhere—to happier times.

"In my youth, I knew loss—however, the gods blessed me with an adult life far beyond what I could ever have dreamed. In Palenque, my sons and my husband were my world, but now I live with tragedy more devastating than before. Although my mother found life unbearable without my father and drank poison to be free from such an existence, I don't have that option."

She paused to wipe the tears from her eyes, and I waited for her to reveal what inspired this strong woman who was once a queen to now willingly live as a slave.

"I will never know if my sons are alive or dead; I can only surmise they did not survive the peasant assault. I will never allow myself to forget their faces or my sweet memories of them. I am grateful I didn't see their fate at the hands of the angry peasants. Chukah took me from the palace before the sacking began. Can you imagine my surprise when he spoke to me then for the first time?"

"Your Majesty, all those years we believed he was mute! It makes me wonder who he really was."

"I have also pondered his true identity since then. He is not like us, you know. His size made him different, of course, but his eyes, his skin … I believe he came from someplace far away." She paused. "Before he took me away from Palenque … he raped me, Itz'At." She closed her eyes as if trying to erase the memory.

"What? How could he have committed such a horrifying act … and against the very person who was the kindest to him?"

"The idea for this unspeakable encounter was implanted in his mind. He told me how he had heard voices his whole life he believed belonged to the Ancestors. But when he was brought to the palace and became my protector, the voices began telling him that I was to be the mother of the new race of Mayas. On our journey here, he revealed Ah Kan Mai's plan to take over Palenque's rule. The high priest had threatened and drugged him to do his bidding, which was to rape me so that Ah Kan Mai could have me sacrificed. But Chukah's act was planned years before Ah Kan Mai's devious plans were formed. Chukah begged my forgiveness—which I granted. Over the many days we traveled to come here, we talked about his life and of the things he observed in Palenque.

"He told me that as a child, he decided if he appeared mute to people, perhaps they would ignore him. What Chukah discovered, however, was that people often revealed more about themselves, knowing he could hear them but believing he had no way to pass along their private information.

"This was so with Ah Kan Mai. That priest's self-image was greatly inflated, and he would often divulge his plans aloud in Chukah's presence, thinking Chukah was under the influence of the opiates he was given."

Chanil hugged her shawl tighter around her thin arms as she remembered something. "Chukah told me that Ah Kan Mai had taken all of Palenque's codices and had them hidden in the mountains by *Puuc* traders. I wonder if we'll ever know where they are. He even disclosed to Chukah that it was he who planned my death on our trip to the cities of

Toniná and Chinkultic. It was the poor, irresponsible son of Toniná's high priest who attempted to push me into the *cenote* at Chinkultic. I doubt anyone ever knew what happened to that unfortunate young man.

"Along the journey here, we traded information with two of Palenque's soldiers who chose to abandon the city with their families as soon as the sacking began. They encountered fleeing peasants who told them about the planned revolt and described the attack on the palace. Most of the people scattered—some to the mountains—but most fled to neighboring cities to begin new lives."

"Were you ever recognized on your journey, My Queen?"

"Oh, no, Itz'At. Thankfully, at all of my public appearances in Palenque, I wore my queen's costumes, body paint, and large headdresses. In fact, Chukah garnered more attention than I did on the road. I was only a simple woman traveling with a huge man."

"You could never be mistaken for simple, Your Majesty!" I countered.

"I am grateful he got me to Chichen Itzá safely. After I obtained work and a home here at the palace, I never saw Chukah again. I have heard he is hard at work in the stone quarries."

"Still, Lady Chanil, what he did was horrible. How you must hate him!"

"I truly believe he acted on beliefs about his destiny—and perhaps somewhat on behalf of the evil Ah Kan Mai. I hold no anger toward him for his drugged actions."

She paused, fingering the plain white tunic she wore. This plainly dressed woman still carried the regal posture of a queen. She struggled to find words.

"The day before the fall of Palenque, Captain Keh Cahal and I grew very close. I realized then I was in love with him. I sincerely loved my husband, the king, but with Keh Cahal, for the first time in my life, I began to feel the true passion lovers feel. I pray his strength as a soldier kept him from the wrath of the peasants.

"I was taken just before the revolt began, yet you were here before me, Itz'At. How did you come to Chichen Itzá?"

"I am embarrassed to say I fled as soon as I heard shouts and smelled smoke. I had heard rumors of peasant unrest and guessed the outcome.

Before I left, I ran to the young princes' room to take them to you to be protected by Chukah. But I saw Keh Cahal going there, so I knew they would be safe with him. I was so wrong to surmise Chukah was protecting you."

The queen's face brightened, color warming her wan cheeks. "You saw Keh Cahal? Perhaps he rescued my sons!"

"We can only hope so. After that, I fled through the escape tunnel beneath the palace and then hid for two nights in the home of my old aunt far outside the palace. She told me how so many of her older women friends agreed to watch the children of the peasants. The parents left them in their care the night of the revolt so they might join in the effort against the monarchy. Although they loved you and the king, the people truly believed their children needed more than the meager existence they lived. Did you know it was Chukah's father who led the revolt?"

"No, Itz'At! I don't think Chukah knew that either."

I paused to serve Lady Chanil another cup of warm tea. "After I left my aunt's home, I journeyed uninterrupted. A lone traveler can make quicker time, so I hardly stopped to sleep on the way. I came here because Chichen Itzá is a large and powerful city. I hoped my skills could be put to use in the palace. I am a coward, My Queen, and now deserve to live disguised as a woman and do women's work. I am so sorry about everything, Your Majesty."

"I am glad you escaped, Itz'At. It was the wish of the gods. And I think you have enough respect for women to know we are strong and resourceful. The work you do here is respected. The life of a woman is very important—at least we women recognize that!" A hint of a smile crossed her face.

"But in the end, no one could have changed what happened to Palenque. I know it wasn't only the workers who destroyed our beautiful city," she said as the sadness returned. "It was all of us. We took everything our land gave—and then more. We took all our peasants had to give and then demanded more. We didn't take care of our beautiful children, and we let them exist undernourished and sick. Itz'At, all of us failed to see the end coming."

"Yes, Your Majesty, even I—who was privy to many meetings with the king, the priests, and the people—couldn't see the direction the city was headed. Or perhaps I just refused to accept it. We all turned away from the signs; we refused to see the truth."

"Palenque's visible wealth and beauty was as fragile as a fine pottery vase," Chanil continued. "She looked exquisite on the outside for all to observe, but was empty on the inside, with no substance—nothing to brace the crushing fate that was to destroy her. I heard that Tikal has suffered the same doom, as will all the great cities of the Mayan Empire," she said, fighting the tears once again forming. "I have also heard it whispered that Toniná has now taken over Palenque. But even they will fall one day."

"Will our people learn from our past mistakes?" I asked hopefully.

"I think not. Palenque's fate is that of every great city unless the people nurture the earth and one another—as we have always nurtured the holy corn." Queen Chanil paused as if struggling to speak again.

"Itz'At, I am with child. I do not know if the baby I carry was fathered by the man I now love or the giant man I once trusted. Chukah could not have known I might possibly have become pregnant by Keh Cahal. My dreams tell me I carry a daughter in my womb. When this child is born, I will teach her to learn from the past, even though the future rests in the hands of the gods. She may be the beginning of a new Maya people. She is the reason I must go on. The gods have given me a new life to live for, and I believe they will guide me forward. I don't know what my future holds, but the gods have also now given me a reason to hope.

"I trust you to tell this tale so that others may heed our lessons. My wish is that future civilizations will not suffer the same fate and will learn from the glory that was Palenque."

Queen Chanil and I talked often after that, and I came to understand her soul as I do my own. I have recorded here all I know of Palenque, the lives of the people, and of the great king and queen who were the last rulers there.

Signed, Itz'At, scribe to King Akal Balam and Queen Chanil Nab Chel of Palenque

ABOUT THE AUTHOR

Dolly Calderon Wiseman was born in San Diego, California. After years performing at local theaters, including the Old Globe and San Diego Civic Light Opera, she married and moved to Los Angeles to pursue an acting career. She found raising her boys most rewarding and spent the next two decades as a wife and mother of three very creative sons.

The memory dream Dolly had in 1980 piqued her interest in the ancient Maya civilization, and she spent the next thirty years researching how the Mayas lived and what might have led to their collapse.

Turning her interests in art and theater to writing, Dolly published a children's story cookbook in 2006 entitled *Everybody Eats Tortillas*. It achieved the publisher's Editor's Choice and Reader's Choice status. She has many more children's cookbooks brewing in her head, but this adult novel had to be told first.

Today, Dolly lives in Calabasas, California with her second husband, Brad. She works in real estate with Brad and enjoys cooking for and entertaining their combined family of five adult kids.

MAYA PRONUNCIATION

A   *ah*

C   hard *k*

Ch   *ch'*

E   *eh*

I   *ee*

J   *h*

O   *oh*

T   *th*

Tz   *dz*

U   *oo*

X   *sh*

'   glottal stop

Stress is usually placed on the last syllable of most words.

CHARACTER NAMES

Ix Chanil Nab Chel	Ix (lady) Chanil (celestial) Nab (water lily) Chel (rainbow)—Queen of Palenque
King Akal Balam	Akal (sea turtle) Balam (jaguar)—King of Palenque
Keh Cahal	Keh (stag) Cahal (place where two waters join)—General of Palenque's army
Men Lamat	Men (wise one; also bird of prey) Lamat (rabbit)—priest and uncle to Queen Chanil
Chukah Nuk T'zi	Chukah (captured) Nuk (large) T'zi (dog)—servant to Queen Chanil
Ah Kan Mai	Ah (holy) Kan (snake) Mai (sun)—High Priest of Palenque
K'in Balam	K'in (prophet) Balam (jaguar)—first son of Akal and Chanil
Chan K'ayum	Chan (little) K'ayum (god of song)—second son of Akal and Chanil
Ix Sak Ayi'in	Ix (lady) Sak (resplendent) Ayi'in (caiman)—sister of Queen Chanil
Cab Men Tun	Cab (earth) Men (wise) Tun (year, stone)—husband of Sak Ayi'in
Ix Zac Ku	Ix (lady) Zac (white) Ku (owl)—First Wife of King Akal
Ix Yax Koh	Ix (lady) Yax (first; also the color deep green) Koh (tooth; also the ceremonial name for the peccary, a wild pig)—daughter of Lady Zac Ku

Na' Nuxi Ku	Na' (mother) Nuxi (ancient one) Ku (owl—associated with fortune-telling)—palace fortuneteller
Itz'At	(artist; scribe; one who is clever, artistic)—palace scribe
Moch Chuen	Moch (scaffold) Chuen (monkey)—adoptive father of Chukah Nuk T'zi
Muluc	servant to Lady Chanil
Mu'ut Ek	servant to Lady Yax Koh

GLOSSARY

ak'ot ahau	sacred dance by the king for his son
ahau	most esteemed ruler
ah k'u hun	keeper of the royal archives
ba'ah ch'ok	first sprout
Baakal, bak	bone
balché	fermented bark and honey drink consumed by the upper class
bat	stonecutter's hatchet
baktun	twenty years
bin in kah	formal goodbye; by your leave
bol	war board game soldiers played
cacao	pod containing seeds to make chocolate
cenote	naturally formed pool used for sacrificial offerings
Cha'ac	rain god
chac	priest who assists in the rain god ceremony
chac chac	ceremony to the rain god
chac mool	sacrificial stone platform
chapat	poisonous centipede
chechem tree	used for its poisonous properties
ch'en	cave; vagina
chibil chin	the "sun's bite"; eclipse
chilan	fortune-teller
cib	vulture
Cincalco	Home of the Maize, similar to purgatory
codex	Maya folded bark paper book
codices	Maya books (plural)
col	cornfield

cutz	turkey
ebet	ambassador
Ek Chuah	god of cocoa trees
glyph	Maya written character representing a word
halach uinic	hereditary ruler
hachas	ball–player's padding
holcans-okot	warrior's dance
holcan	foot soldier
ichca huipil	quilted cotton or palm fiber armor covered in deer hide
ik	wind; breath
ik'al cacao	chocolate drink with ground-up pink and white cacao blossoms
Itzamná	highest progenitor god, first priest, and patron of writing and the divinatory arts
Itzám Nah	sacred underground house of the priests
Ix Chel	the Lady Rainbow, goddess of women's work and childbirth, nurse protector, midwife, warrior
k'antuun	yellow limestone
katun	ten years
K'awiil	patron god of the Maya lineage, god of fertility; sperm
kayuk	kayak, small boat
k'in	one day
k'inyah	psychic gifts
ko'ox	we march; let's go
k'uk	most colorful and revered bird of the jungle; also known as quetzal
k'ulel	holy energy
kunul	conjuring place
lac	sacred offertory bowl
Lakam Ha	big water
Lo'K'in	mythical cannibal survivors from the age of Wooden Men
manzanas	a measurement of land
mas	dwarf

molé	spicy ground sauce made of chili pepper and chocolate
metate	grinding surface of clay or stone
Mik' chal uh	young girl's rites of adulthood
nacom	war chief
nauyaca	pit viper found in the cornfields
nehn	mirror used for divination
patí	cape
pib nah	steam bath house
pitz	ball court
pitzlawal	ball players, athletes
plom	merchant
pom	flammable and fragrant incense made from sap of the copal tree used in ceremonies
pooxah	leather pouch
Popol Na	palace building with open court
po't	women's simple white under-gown, shift
posol	cornmeal drink
Puuc	foreign traders and boat pilots who traded goods and information
sab'ak	soot
sacbé	white road
sac hunal	white headband worn by royalty
sahal	man of power, regional governor
sak'al	army ants of the jungle
ta'	feces
tax	drum
Tok Tan	Cloud Center Valley
Tomoanchan	a place of existence prior to reincarnation
T'o'ohil	ancient people believed to have come from the heavens to teach the Mayas
tun	365 days; stone
tup	earplug
tzab	rattlesnake tail
tzuk	province
uay	spirit animal guide
uinal	approximately one month

unen	newborn
Uayeb	the last five unlucky days of a year
wakahchan	mythical ceiba tree believed to reach both the heavens and the underworld
x'man	shaman, healer, priest
xibalbá	Maya afterlife
xikul	men's woven cotton tunic
Xoc	mythical mermen/shark men believed to lure women into water and drown them
Yah'ak Ah	god of hunters and archers
yahau	political gathering
yat	penis
Yax Tun	green stone; jade boulder
yitz'in	brother
Yum Chom	god of the vultures
Yum Kaax	god of the maize
zabcán	rattlesnake
Zac Nuk Na	white skin house; Palenque's only white holy building

16388980R00130

Printed in Great Britain
by Amazon